It was our first real kiss . . .

Without saying another word Danny leaned his head forward and kissed me. At first I was kind of surprised—stunned, I should say—and didn't know how to react. Fortunately, my lips quickly took over. It was our first real kiss—my first real kiss—and it was just like in the movies—it went on and on and on.

D1513074

Collect every Changes Romance

My Phantom Love
Looking Out for Lacey
The Unbelievable Truth
Runaway
Cinderella Summer
Wild Hearts
Can't Buy Me Love
Choose Me*
My Sister's Boyfriend*

And don't miss

Freshman Dorm—the Hit Series!
by Linda A. Cooney
Now twenty titles strong!

*coming soon

A *Changes* ROMANCE

CAN'T BUY ME LOVE

MALLORY STEVENS

HarperPaperbacks

A Division of HarperCollinsPublishers

This is a work of fiction. The characters, incidents, and dialogues are products of the author's imagination and are not to be construed as real. Any resemblance to actual events or persons, living or dead, is entirely coincidental.

HarperPaperbacks *A Division of* HarperCollins*Publishers*
10 East 53rd Street, New York, N.Y. 10022

Produced by Daniel Weiss Associates, Inc., 33 West 17th Street, New York, New York 10011.

First printing: September, 1992

Printed in the United States of America

HarperPaperbacks and colophon are trademarks of HarperCollins*Publishers*

10 9 8 7 6 5 4 3 2 1

Dear Reader,

Thanks for picking up this Changes Romance. We hope that you'll enjoy reading it as much as we've enjoyed bringing it to you.

Our goal is to present realistic stories about girls in true-to-life circumstances, with relationships and problems that readers will understand and appreciate. In other words, we want to try to capture the changes you're probably facing in your own life today.

We hope we've succeeded, but the only way we can know for sure is to hear from you. Please write us or your favorite Changes authors, and tell us what you liked (or didn't like!) about the Changes Romances you've read. Tell us how we stack up against your other favorite books. Tell us about the kinds of stories you'd like to read in future Changes novels: What does romance mean to you? What kinds of characters do you identify with? Where should the stories take place? What sort of problems or conflicts should a Changes heroine encounter? In this way, we can bring you more of the stories *you* want to read.

Again, thanks for reading this Changes Romance. Our address is printed below. We hope you'll look for the new Changes Romance each month, and we hope to hear from you very soon.

Sincerely,

Chloë Nichols

Chloë Nichols
Editor
Daniel Weiss Associates, Inc.
33 West 17th Street
New York, N.Y. 10011

For Michelle and Jason Edelman,
with love.
And for Claremont Riding Academy,
the most magical place in Manhattan.

CAN'T BUY ME LOVE

CHAPTER

ONE

This morning was a perfect New York City morning. The sun was shining, and we had our first break in the awful summer humidity. It made me almost want to stay in the city—almost!

As usual, my mom and I were running late. Even though the yellow cab managed to magically weave its way through the crowded streets, by the time it screeched to a stop in front of Penn Station, I was positive I'd miss my train.

Mom had tried to make small talk during the cab ride, but I was too anxious

1

about what lay ahead of me to do more than grunt in response to her questions. Finally, she gave up and we spent the rest of the ride staring out the windows and listening to the cabdriver sing along to the music on the radio.

I watched the rush-hour traffic crawl by as the cabbie unloaded my luggage. My mom seemed to take forever to pay him when he was done, and I shifted impatiently from foot to foot.

"Mom! Come on," I urged. "I have to go!"

Finally she collected her change and stepped out of the cab. I threw my knapsack over my right shoulder, grabbed my duffel bag in my left hand, and headed into the huge building.

"Do you have your ticket?" Mom yelled after me. I was walking at top speed toward the information booth.

"For the millionth time, it's in my jacket pocket," I yelled over my shoulder. In spite of my confident words, I quickly patted the pocket just to make sure.

When I got to the counter, I was completely out of breath. I readjusted the bags and waited for my turn in line. The line crawled as I finally reached the woman behind the glass enclosure.

"Can you tell me on what track the train for Ithaca is leaving?"

The heavyset woman picked up a clipboard and ran her finger up and down the chart a couple of times. She barely glanced up as she said, "It's Track Twelve. Over there." She gestured over her shoulder toward the end of the terminal. "You'd better hurry, though. It's scheduled to pull out in less than five minutes."

"Thanks," I called out, hurrying toward Track 12 with my mom just two steps behind. In a way, I was glad we were running late. It meant less time for long, tearful good-byes. I knew that given half a chance, Mom was going to get really soppy. And the last thing I needed was more tears! I had done enough crying this summer. I didn't think my eyes could take any more.

When Mom and I reached the first car of the train, I handed my ticket to the porter. "Can you tell me where my seat is?" I asked him.

He looked at the ticket and then said, "You're in the fourth car from the rear, window seat. Let me help you with those bags."

I was really glad to turn over my duffel bag to the porter. I had tried to pack light but had failed miserably. Even though I was planning to come home from college over Thanksgiving vacation partly to get more of my stuff, my bag was stuffed to the top.

The porter took the duffel bag from me and picked up the large suitcase that Mom had been carrying. We followed the porter to the fourth car and climbed aboard. The porter led the way to my seat and then put the large bags in the overhead rack before turning back to me.

"Is there anything else I can get you, miss?" he asked.

"No, thanks," I replied.

"Well, have a good trip." He tipped his cap and started back down the car.

My mom followed him for a few steps. I smiled to myself as I saw her stop the porter and give him a ten-dollar bill. She leaned close to him and whispered in his ear.

"Keep an eye on her, will you? This is her first time away from home," she said quietly, but not so quietly that I couldn't hear her.

Normally when my mom does stuff like that, you know, treats me like a little kid, it embarrasses me. But not this time. I felt strangely comforted by her obvious caring. I guess we both knew that I wasn't going to be getting much mothering for a while.

The porter smiled broadly and said, "Yes, ma'am, don't worry. I'll make sure she gets there safe and sound." Then he tipped his cap and continued down the aisle, whistling to himself.

I was busy going through my knapsack when Mom returned. I pretended that I hadn't seen the exchange between her and the porter as I removed my Walkman and some of my favorite tapes and placed them on the empty seat next to me. Then I put the knapsack up in the overhead rack and turned toward Mom, who was, as I predicted, starting to cry.

"Well, I guess I'd better be going. You sure you have everything? Is there anything else you need?" she said as she tried to hold back her tears.

"No, Mom," I said. "I've got all I need. Thanks . . . thanks for everything," I said as I hugged and kissed her.

"Now don't forget to call me as soon as you get up to the dorm," she said as she quickly wiped at her eyes. "Darn! I promised myself I wouldn't cry . . . not after all the tears we've shed this summer."

I tried to smile but failed miserably. I had lost the battle for dry eyes myself.

"Mom, please stop," I begged in a choked voice. "We said we weren't going to cry, didn't we?"

Mom nodded her head "yes" before taking a deep breath. "Well, I have to get to the office. Mr. Demarko was nice enough to give me the morning off, but I don't want to take advantage of him."

I nodded, too choked up now to speak.

"I know this was supposed to have been the best summer of your life," Mom continued. "I'm sorry it didn't turn out that way. Just remember that I love you very much and that I'm very proud of you."

As she said this I felt the tears begin to stream down my face. Mom and I hugged one last time before she dabbed my eyes and her own.

"Oh, here's a little extra spending money. Have a good dinner tonight when you get to Ithaca." She pushed some folded-up bills into my hand before turning and hurrying down the aisle and out the door.

I stared after her and then watched her through the windows of the train as she walked back up the platform. I took a deep breath and sat down before I looked at the money Mom had given me. I had four folded fifty-dollar bills in my hand.

I couldn't believe it! Mom didn't make tons of money, and two hundred dollars would put a serious dent in her finances.

I started to rise from the seat to go after her, but the train lurched and slowly began pulling out of the station through the underground maze of tunnels that would eventually lead to daylight . . . and to a whole new life for me.

I sat back down and stared at the walls of the station as the train began picking up speed. Before long, the speed of the train made it difficult for me to make out the individual columns that supported the tunnel. They flashed by in a blur of dirty white tiles.

Suddenly, the train emerged from the darkness into the sunlight of early September. Even through the tinted windows, the bright light caused me to squint and I shielded my eyes with my hand.

As my eyes grew accustomed to the intensity of the light, I thought again about how quickly things can change. But this time, for the first time, the thought of change was exciting, not terrifying. Maybe it was because I know now that I have the confidence to handle whatever happens.

Is it only September? I thought. *It seems as if all those terrible, agonizing times happened years ago, not weeks ago.* But they *had* only started in June . . . right after graduation.

I slowly shook my head. What had seemed so far away only a moment ago, now seemed like only yesterday. . . .

CHAPTER

TWO

I live in New York City, the greatest city in the world. It has everything anyone could want—the best restaurants, the best entertainment, the best stores, the best everything! The only *real* problem with New York is that with the exception of a few days a year, the weather is terrible!

New York can be particularly gross in the summer. The air is usually so thick and heavy that even walking down the street is an effort. But on that day in early June—the day when everything really started—the air was crisp and clear, the sun was bright, and there was a breeze blowing off the Hudson River. It was enough to make anyone happy just to be alive.

I was sitting on the front steps of Parkside Stables with my best friend, Susan Goldman, and our three other friends at the stables, Denise Cole, Penny Thomas, and Laura Harris.

Susan is younger than the rest of us. She's only fifteen, but she can ride a horse, *any* horse, and make it look incredibly easy. At the time, Susan was also the only one of the five of us who didn't own her own horse.

Denise, Penny, and Laura each had a really expensive thoroughbred horse— and I had Mirage. I used to think that Mirage was my real best friend, not Susan, but even I realized that the most wonderful horse in the world has limitations. I mean, can you imagine going to the movies or shopping or getting a burger with a horse?

Even though Susan is my best friend now, that wasn't always the case. Until recently, that is until my dad left, I mostly hung around with Denise, Penny, and Laura. We all went to a private school in Manhattan and we all had horses at Parkside.

Susan went to a public school near the stable, as I did *after* my parents got their divorce. Back when I was ten and Susan was eight, a couple of years seemed to be a bigger deal than it is now that I am seventeen and Susan, fifteen.

Though all five of us continued to hang out at the stable together, once I stopped going to a private school and living in a big apartment, I had less in common with the others and more in common with Susan.

At first, right after the divorce, I felt really bad about the way my life had changed. No more expensive clothes, fancy restaurants, and exotic vacations. But before long, I realized that we were actually better off than we had been. Mom was happier without all the yelling and fighting and arguing, and so was I. Besides, I still had Mirage.

Anyway, that morning back in June the five of us had gone riding in Central Park. We were all feeling pretty good by the time we got back to Parkside. As far as I was concerned, no matter *what* was going on, life was wonderful when viewed from the back of Mirage. It was really the only time I *did* feel life was wonderful. When I wasn't on Mirage, I spent too much time thinking about the things I didn't have. And worse than that, I felt so alone.

I guess the "thing" I didn't have the most was someone special in my life, someone I could totally trust. I guess I knew that as great as my mom is, she had her own problems to deal with, and even before the divorce I just didn't want to add my problems to hers.

Anyway, during the winter we all hung out on the mounting block inside of the barn, but when spring arrived the steps seemed the place to be. As usual we were talking about our favorite subject . . . guys! For me, the discussions were mostly "wishful thinking." Oh sure, there were guys whom I talked to at school. I mean I wasn't totally *unexposed* to them, but I had never found one I really wanted to get close to. I don't know if it was the boys I had to choose from or if it was me, if I were just too picky. At times, though, I thought that maybe Susan was right when she said I was just too scared.

So we were chatting about guys and horses and more guys when Mr. Booth, the farrier, pulled up in his truck. Mr. Booth is a tall, gray-haired man; I've known him ever since I started riding at Parkside. Most of the other girls think Mr. Booth is mean. He yells and carries on when one of the girls neglects her horse, but I know he's really an old softy. He just wants the horses taken care of properly and that, after all, *is* the owner's responsibility.

Mr. Booth comes to Parkside three times a week to make sure that the shoes on the horses' feet are in good shape and that none of the horses are showing symptoms of lameness.

Nobody took much notice at first— Mr. Booth is hardly anyone's idea of a conversation stopper—but when a totally gorgeous young guy stepped out of the truck, we all shut up. The guy was tall and muscular and tan. And he had the blondest hair, the whitest teeth, and the most perfect smile I had ever seen. I swear my heart stopped beating when he looked in my direction.

"Dibs on him!" Susan and I said together. We looked at each other and collapsed into giggles. The others didn't think our remark was all that funny.

"Gross!" Denise stuck her nose in the air. "A farrier's helper? Come on, Julia, you can't be serious."

"Actually," Penny said, in a whisper loud enough to be heard across the street, "I think that's Mr. Booth's son, Danny."

Laura just shook her blond curls. "Gee, Julia, maybe you two could get together and he could take you some place really nice . . . like a hot-dog stand or a ball game!"

Denise and Penny broke out in laughter. *I* didn't think Laura's comment was very funny and I just sat there turning red. Those girls were the "in" crowd at Parkside; and at the time I was dumb enough to think that they were somehow always *right* because of that.

I don't know whether I gave as much weight to their opinions when I had been one of them, part of their elitist club, but after my life changed—after the divorce and all that—the things those three thought and said took on a whole new level of importance to me. I knew my position as one of the "in" crowd was sort of tenuous, and I didn't want to lose my grip. Those girls were my only contact with my old way of life.

"Come on, Julia," Susan said, grabbing my arm, "let's go get Mirage and have his shoes checked out."

"Perfect!" Denise snorted. *"Danny* can check out Mirage's shoes, while you're checking out Danny. Very smooth!"

Susan and I left the three of them on the steps, making fun of us, no doubt.

Parkside is an old carriage house that was built back around the turn of the century. The main floor is now an arena with a mounting block in the corner.

The horses are stabled either "upstairs" or "downstairs." We should say "Up Ramp" or "Down Ramp," which would be more precise, but we don't. Anyway, all the boarders have their horses upstairs in twelve-by-twelve-foot box stalls.

In spite of their laughter, I noticed the

three other girls had followed us upstairs and were getting their horses ready to go downstairs to be checked by Mr. Booth. Susan went with me to get Mirage.

My stall was a few stalls away from the others', so Susan and I couldn't quite hear what Denise, Laura, and Penny were saying. We could hear them chuckling, though, and I knew that they were still laughing at Susan and me.

Susan must have seen me turn bright red, because she put her hand on my arm. "I can't believe you let those snobs on saddles get to you!"

I had to laugh hearing "snobs on saddles" come out of Susan's mouth. That was as close as she's probably ever gotten to swearing. Susan's tiny, so any sort of nasty language coming from her mouth sounds kind of silly. I think that's why she said it, to cheer me up.

Susan handed me Mirage's halter. It's a nice one made of braided leather. It was the last gift my father gave me before he left for California with *her*, his new wife. Mom and I don't ever say *her* name. We don't talk about my dad much, either.

Sometimes Susan and I talked about

my dad, though. Because I couldn't talk about him with my mom and I didn't *really* talk to anyone else about serious stuff at all, Susan was the only one I *could* talk to about him.

The only nice thing I can say about my dad now is that he gave me Mirage. Maybe that's saying a lot. It was my eighth birthday and I had been riding for about two years. My dad had taken me to the stable for my usual Saturday lesson. My instructor had told me there was a new horse she wanted me to ride. It was Mirage. We, that is Mirage and I, had clicked immediately. I seemed to know exactly what he was going to do before he did it, and he seemed to know just what I wanted him to do before I asked him to.

After that first lesson with Mirage, I ran over to my dad and told him how much I loved the little white Arabian gelding.

"That's good," he'd said with a grin, "because he's all yours. Happy Birthday, Pumpkin!" That's probably the clearest memory of my dad I have. It's certainly the happiest.

By the time Susan and I got downstairs, the other three girls were already outside with their horses. None of the horses was tacked up yet. That is, none of them had on saddles or bridles. Just halters. It was a sight that never failed to interest me. Four horses, their coats gleaming in the sun against the backdrop of Manhattan's skyscrapers. Kind of a weird contrast, you know?

Mr. Booth works out of his truck. It's really a mobile shoeing station, complete with a forge to heat the horseshoes so that they can be molded to fit the horse's hooves exactly.

Penny was, as always, first. Mr. Booth worked on her horse's hind legs while Danny looked at Laura's horse, Money's, left front shoe.

"Are you sure you've done this before?" Laura asked Danny. "I mean, like, Money is a very expensive animal. I wouldn't want anything to go wrong!"

I could never understand how those other girls could refer to their horses as "animals." *My* horse was so much more. Mirage was my closest confidant, my buddy. I don't know how I could have gotten through the divorce without him. When my parents were fighting, or after my dad left and Mom would be in her room crying, I would sneak out of the apartment and go down to the stable and sit with Mirage. I did most of my crying in Mirage's stall. The only happy memories I have of that time were those hours I spent with my horse. I would *never* have referred to him as just an *animal*. I couldn't have.

"Don't worry," Danny said, his voice deep and soothing. "I'll be very careful."

I looked over and was surprised by the twinkle in his blue eyes. He was saying all the right things to Laura, but the twinkle made it clear that he thought she was acting like a jerk.

"Okay." Laura sniffed. "Go ahead."

Danny checked the rest of Money's shoes. They must not have needed to be taken off and changed. He poked around them a bit before finishing with Money and turning to Denise to ask her if she wanted him to look at her horse. Denise, of course, said she would rather wait for Mr. Booth to examine *her* horse.

As I mentioned before, it was a

beautiful, breezy day, but when Danny turned to look at me, I swear the temperature suddenly went up about a million degrees. I could feel myself instantly start to sweat.

"I'll be with you in a sec," he said, smiling at me. He turned back to the truck and all of a sudden peeled off his T-shirt. He turned back to me. "It's hot near the forge," he added by way of an explanation.

I felt like a total idiot. All I could do was stand there and gape. Lucky for me, Susan shoved me forward—hard.

"I'm hot, too," I said as I stumbled toward him a couple of steps. I desperately wanted to die. What an unbelievably dumb thing to say! I closed my eyes as I felt myself go red all over again.

"You look it," I heard Danny say. "You're all flushed." It wasn't exactly high praise, but, well, it *did* come from the most incredible hunk I'd ever met.

Unlike the others—not counting Susan because she's still a bit young—I had never even come close to having a boyfriend. Due to my inexperience, I have to admit that at that moment, standing that close to an eighteen-year-old guy with a great body wearing no shirt *did* make me a bit uncomfortable. Did I say uncomfortable? I was absolutely *panicked*, but I took a couple of deep breaths and quickly got ahold of myself.

Danny already had one of Mirage's legs propped up on his knee. "The front shoes look okay," he observed. "Let's see how the back ones look."

"Need some help?" Susan volunteered enthusiastically. She looked at me and smiled broadly.

Susan could be such a pain! Mr. Booth and the other girls had gone inside by this time, so it was just the three of us still standing outside.

Susan looked at me and raised her eyebrows as if to say "Should I go away?" I shook my head.

"What's wrong?" Danny asked.

"Huh? Oh, nothing! Why?" It wasn't exactly a bright reply, but it was the best I could come up with just then.

"Well, you just shook your head. Don't you want me to check the hind shoes?"

"No! I mean yes! I *do* want you to

21

check them." *Great*, I thought grimly. *Now he thinks I'm a total creep!*

Way back then, in early June, other people's opinions of me practically ruled my life. One of the big things I learned this summer was to stop worrying about what other people think of me. I learned about trust: trusting myself so that the opinions of people I don't respect don't matter so much, and trusting other people, the people I *do* respect. It was a hard lesson. Let's face it, before this summer, I hadn't really had much positive experience in trusting other people.

"No new shoes needed today," he announced as he set Mirage's left hind leg gently back on the cement.

I was relieved. "Good. That's one less expense to worry about," I said.

Danny laughed. It didn't sound like a nice laugh, and it took me by surprise. "I thought girls like you didn't worry about trivial things like bills. Doesn't Daddy just take care of them?" There was an edge to his voice that made me angry.

"I don't happen to have a *daddy*!" I snapped. "And, as if it's any of your business, I don't know what you mean by 'girls like you.' I'm *not* a little rich girl."

We glared at each other for a moment without speaking. I completely forgot about Susan or Mirage or anything else that was going on around us. I could feel the tears begin to well up in my eyes. Then his gaze softened.

"I'm sorry," he said, smiling at me. That smile had an unbelievable effect on me . . . I turned into total mush. It was a smile that could make anyone forget and forgive anything.

"It's okay," I said a bit coolly. Of course, I'd already forgiven him, but I wasn't ready to let him know that he was off the hook.

He stuck out his hand. "Look, I apologize. I was out of line. Danny Booth, big mouth, at your service."

Now I had to smile, too. Especially because behind Danny's back Susan was doing an exaggerated pantomime of tiptoeing away to leave us alone.

"Julia Morgan, hothead, at yours." I took his hand. It was large and calloused from his work. I stopped breathing as I felt the strength in his grip. I never wanted to let go!

Mirage started to paw the ground as if he wanted to get in on the introductions. I dropped Danny's hand and patted Mirage on the neck. "And this is Mirage Morgan, my pride and joy. Mirage, say hello to Danny."

Danny reached into his pocket and pulled out a lump of sugar to feed to Mirage. "He's a real beauty. An Arabian, right? About twelve years old?"

I felt a thrill go through me. I had always been a total sucker for anyone who admired my horse. "Yep. Actually, he's almost thirteen. I've had him for about nine years." I started to rub Mirage's "scratch spot."

Horses have this one place on their necks that they love to have scratched. If you get the spot just right, they stick their necks straight out, flatten their ears back on their heads, and wiggle their big lips. It's a pleasure reflex, just like when you tickle a dog and its hind leg starts to shake. Mirage started to do that right in Danny's face.

"He doesn't feel a thing, does he?"

Danny said, laughing at the way Mirage's lips wiggled. "Does it have the same effect on you?" He reached out as though he was going to start tickling my neck.

I was blushing like crazy just as Mr. Booth came out of the office. "Danny, let's go! We have to be out in Jersey before two o'clock." Danny waved to his dad and turned back to me. The moment for tickling had obviously passed, and I was kind of disappointed. "I'll be checking on Mirage," Danny said, *"and* you, when I come back next week. See 'ya."

Before I could blush *again* or say something I would regret for the rest of my life, I blurted out, "Bye." Then, leading Mirage, I turned and jogged into the safety and cool darkness of the arena.

Once my eyes adjusted to the relative gloom, I could see that Susan wasn't at her usual place on the mounting block. I ran up the ramp with Mirage following me.

One of my favorite things about Mirage is the fact that I don't usually have to attach a lead rope to his halter. He follows me like a puppy . . . a very *large* puppy!

As I suspected, Susan was up in Mirage's stall. Aside from being a really sweet person, Susan has one outstanding character trait. She loves my horse. That's why, even though I knew I was going to miss Mirage beyond belief when I went away to college in the fall, I also knew he'd be happy here with Susan.

When I had been accepted to college, Mom and I had a long talk. I'd really hated my father that day, because with money tight, it was my tuition or Mirage's keep. We just couldn't afford both. It was that simple. Mom told me that when I left for school, I was going to have to give up Mirage. There was no other way.

The other girls at Parkside who were going away to college all planned on taking their horses with them. I could barely afford to feed and board myself, so I could forget about taking Mirage along.

I hated the idea of selling Mirage to some stranger and didn't know what I was going to do. That's why when Susan said that she'd pay for Mirage's board if I left him at Parkside, it seemed like a perfect solution.

Susan's family doesn't have much money, either, but she figured that if she put all the money she'd made in the last year baby-sitting, walking dogs, and working around the stable into a savings account, she'd be able to pay Mirage's board. She hasn't been able to go to the movies a lot in the last few months or to buy too many new clothes, but she really wants to be able to keep Mirage. I want her to be able to as well, so I've been giving her a few bucks for the account whenever I can.

Susan was cleaning out, or "mucking," Mirage's stall when I came flying in talking a mile a minute.

"So then, when he started rubbing Mirage and looking at me, I couldn't believe it! And when he was about to touch my neck, I almost died. He is absolutely the most gorgeous guy I've ever met."

My sentences were all running together. "When his dad called him to go, Danny said 'I'll be back to check on you and Mirage.' What do you think that means?"

Susan, who was knee-deep in horse droppings, looked up with a thoughtful expression. After pausing for a moment she said, "I guess it means that he's coming back to check on Mirage's shoes."

"Su-sa-an!" She was being so dense!

"Well, maybe it means he has fallen in love with you." Susan started to laugh. "He wants to get married and have a family with four children and . . ."

Before she could complete her sentence, I picked up a handful of hay and heaved it at her. She tried to duck but lost her balance and tripped.

From her position on the floor of the stall lying in a pile of hay, Susan looked up at me and said, "This is war!"

Laughing like twelve-year-olds, we both started hurling handfuls of hay. When we were completely covered and declared the war was over, I looked at Susan, who was pulling hay out of her hair and the back of her shirt.

"Seriously," I said, "he didn't have to say 'Mirage and *you.*' He could have just said 'Mirage.'"

"Yeah, I guess so." Susan looked doubtful. "Tell me, would you go out with him?"

I nodded. Just then Denise, Penny, and Laura came around the corner.

"Go out with whom?" Laura asked.

"Danny Booth?" Denise suggested. "Julia thinks he's cute."

I was bright red at this point, but Susan saved me from further embarrassment. "Anybody for a ride?" she asked. "I have to exercise Mr. Martin's new thoroughbred, Thunder."

There are only two things that can distract Denise when she's on the attack—her boyfriend, William Barstow, Jr., or a ride in the park. We all got our horses ready.

To prepare a horse for riding you have to give him at least a little bit of grooming—brush his coat and clean out the mud in his hooves—tack him up—put on his saddle and bridle.

I decided not to put a saddle on Mirage and ride him bareback instead. Staying mounted without a saddle requires balance, courage, a lot of practice, and trust. I really trusted Mirage not to do anything that would result in my being hurt. Even though he was high-spirited, I knew he would never, ever try to throw me.

Susan, on the other hand, was a little nervous as we rode out of Parkside. Riding a new horse, especially one as green as Thunder, is always a bit hazardous.

When you say a horse is "green," it means that he's not very well trained. He's inexperienced, probably a bit unreliable, and likely to shy, back up, or sidestep if he gets frightened, or bolt if he gets the urge. Only an experienced rider, like Susan, would want to take out a horse like that in Central Park.

We rode single file to the park, with Thunder in the middle. He shied a couple of times as the buses went by but was basically okay. When we got to the park, Susan was in charge. Whenever someone is on a green horse, she sets the pace and gait.

Gait means walk, trot, or canter and pace means speed of the gait. Safety is a big concern to everyone who is serious about riding. It is the one thing that none of us fooled around with.

The park was gorgeous—the grass was an unbelievable shade of green, and the trees were in full bloom. You could almost believe that you were in some sort of primeval forest and that the noises of traffic were being made by the weird animals that lived there.

Thunder seemed to be calm, so Susan asked for a slow trot. We all picked it up and rode five abreast. It felt so good to be out with my friends, feeling Mirage beneath me. I remember the air smelled like, well, like freedom!

Since my dad left, I'd always had a part-time job during the summers, but this spring my mother had told me that the summer was her graduation gift to me. She knew how much I was going to miss Mirage in the fall.

I think that even though we didn't really talk about it, Mom knew that Mirage was as good a friend to me as Susan. I guess she wanted me to have these nine weeks between high school and college just to enjoy myself with my two best friends. It was the best present anyone could have given me.

Denise, Laura, and Penny moved ahead by a couple of lengths, so I trotted Mirage closer to Thunder. The other girls' voices floated back to us.

"So I figure Billy and I will move into

an apartment together during our sopho-
more or junior year," Denise was saying.
She had been dating Bill, Jr., for the past
two years. They were both starting at
Yale in the fall, and everyone—including
Denise—assumed they'd get married
right after college.

"Won't your parents freak?" Laura
asked. She came from a pretty strict family.

"Who cares?" Denise asked.

"Are you sure you want to settle down
so soon?" Penny had a one-track mind,
and everyone knew it. "I can't wait to
date all those Ivy League boys!" Denise,
Laura, and Penny had all gone to a really
ritzy private high school. Now they were
all headed to prestigious colleges. Prestigious, private, and *expensive.*

"Don't you mean *men?*" Denise
started to laugh. She turned back and
looked over her shoulder at us. "Is it
okay if we canter ahead of you two, Susan?"

Susan nodded. "But if you hear me
come flying up behind you, stop. Okay?"
Denise threw her a salute and the three
cantered off. It was a little rough for a

few seconds as Thunder, who was only recently off the racetrack, tried to join them at a dead gallop, but Susan showed him that she was in total control.

Horses will often test their riders to see how much they can get away with. Susan wasn't going to let Thunder get away with anything.

"All right, Thunder—easy, boy!" Susan said as she reined back on the big animal. Thunder whinnied but began to settle down. Susan had won that little battle of wills.

"You don't mind just trotting for a while?" she asked me.

"Actually, I wouldn't mind walking," I confessed. "Now I remember why I normally use a saddle. Mirage's back is *so* bony."

With Denise, Laura, and Penny out of our hair, we spent a pleasant hour in the park. We walked a little and trotted a bit. We even did a short, slow canter for a while. But mostly we talked—not about the fall and college and my separation from Mirage, but about the wonderful summer we had ahead of us. And, of course, about Danny!

CHAPTER

THREE

I tend to think about that summer in terms of major events. The rest of the time in between has faded into one long blur. I have vague memories of grooming Mirage, riding Mirage, talking to Mirage —just being with Mirage.

You know that feeling when you wake up in the morning and for a split second can't remember why you're so excited? You know that you are excited, but you're not sure whether it is an "Oh-my-god-I-have-a-test-I-forgot-to-study-for" excitement or an "It's-my-birthday" excitement.

About a week after I first met Danny, I woke up with that feeling. Then I remembered that it was the day when I was going to see him again and I practically flew out of my bed. It was weird. I mean there I was, totally excited about seeing a guy I'd only had one conversation with, one very short conversation. It wasn't like me at all.

Usually, the only thing I really got into was stuff with Mirage. Maybe that's why it was so easy for me to think about Danny in such a positive way. I associated him with Mirage, so I felt comfortable. Well, to be honest, let's say *more* comfortable than I would have otherwise.

Mirage needed new shoes, which meant that not only was I going to see Danny, but I would have a perfectly legitimate reason to spend at least a half hour standing next to him.

I'm usually pretty good in the morning, but that morning I stood at the foot of my bed, breathing hard and not really sure what to do. Finally, I took three deep breaths to calm down; I do the same thing before I enter the ring during a horse show. I caught sight of myself in the mirror and decided that a shower was definitely the first order of the day.

One of the big disadvantages of living on the top floor of an old building in New York City is water pressure—or rather, the lack of water pressure. It takes about five minutes of letting the shower run before the water is consistently one temperature. Then you have to deal with the sudden drops and rises. There's no worse feeling in the world than having your hair all lathered up and then getting hit with a blast of ice-cold water.

I usually wait until the temperature has had a chance to equalize before getting into the shower. But I was in such a rush that morning that I took my chances. Big mistake! But, then again, maybe not. By the time I got out of the bathroom, the alternating hot and cold water had completely cleared my head.

I'm not lucky in a lot of things, but one area where I definitely scored was my hair. It hangs about halfway down my back and is naturally curly. In grade school I hated it and wanted straight hair, but now I'm very happy with it. All I do is run my fingers through it when it's wet and let it dry. A major time-saver. Because it always looks slightly messy anyhow, no one can tell when it really is.

Still wrapped in a towel, I wandered back into my bedroom to get dressed. One of the great things about riding is that you always know what you are going to wear—at least on the bottom half of your body: boots and britches.

I grabbed a new pair of britches from the dresser and took them out of their plastic wrapping. They were a lovely honey color, called canary yellow by those of us in the horse world, and had suede patches on the inside of the knees.

I always got one pair of britches for Christmas and another for the Summer Horse Show. I really was supposed to save the new pair for the show, but you know how it is when you are trying to impress someone . . . especially an incredibly good-looking guy! That was another thing that was kind of strange for me that morning.

I'd never actually tried to impress guys before. In fact, the only man I'd ever shown off for was my dad. And no matter how much I tried, or how much he said he loved me, it wasn't enough to make him stick around. After Dad left, the only member of the opposite sex I was interested in was Mirage. Most of the guys I met didn't think a fun date consisted of hanging out at the stables. If I wanted to be with them, I couldn't hang out with Mirage. I knew, however, that with Danny things were different. I was already anticipating being able to be with him and Mirage at the same time.

I tried on every shirt in my closet—twice. Finally I settled on a pale pink tank top that Susan had told me looked great against my tan. I whistled an old Beatles song that was playing on an oldies station and looked in the mirror one last time. I liked what I saw. I hoped Danny would, too.

I didn't want to wake Mom, so I carried my boots and tiptoed into the kitchen to make a pot of coffee. As it brewed, I sat at the kitchen table trying to spit-polish the worst of the grime off of the once-shiny black leather and thinking about what I was going to say to Danny.

Mom was still in her bathrobe when she came into the kitchen. "Julia, *please* don't clean your boots at the breakfast table."

"Sorry," I said, putting down the boots. I stood up and did a little twirl. "Do I look okay?"

She finished pouring herself a cup of coffee and turned around to look.

"You look great."

One of the things I love most about my mother is that when you ask her a question she doesn't give an automatic "Yes, dear." She actually thinks about things and gives you a real answer. I went over to her and gave her a big hug.

"Aren't those your new britches?" she asked with raised eyebrows.

"Uh, yeah . . ." I stammered.

"Well, you look great, but you know we won't be able to get you another pair for the show if these get ruined."

"I know, Mom." I sat down, feeling

completely deflated. "Believe me, I know."

Mom came over to me, put her hand on my shoulder, and kissed me on the forehead. "I'm sorry. I wish I could afford to get you all those things the other girls have, but . . ." Her voice trailed off.

I knew what she really meant. She didn't care about the other girls. She meant "all those thing you *used* to have when your dad was around."

I guess I should explain a bit about my family and about what happened to us. First of all, we used to be a real family with a mother, a father, and a kid—me. Things were fine for a long time. Then Mom and my dad started fighting. I didn't know what it was all about, and that made things difficult for me. I thought I was the problem, that my parents' unhappiness was my fault.

When I finally found out what the real problem was, it turned out to be worse than anything I'd imagined. My dad was cheating on my mom. With his secretary. I realized that my dad wasn't who I thought he was. I couldn't trust him at all. Then he told Mom that he needed to "find himself"—whatever that meant.

What it meant to us—Mom and me—was that he was leaving us. And when he left, he left us with nothing. I couldn't believe it when it happened, but now we're on our own.

Even now, almost two years later, I still sometimes feel that it was all a weird dream. I mean if you can't trust your own dad, whom can you trust? I hadn't really bothered to try to find out since he left. I never had a reason to . . . until now . . . until I met Danny.

Right after the divorce was official, Mom took back her maiden name. She's Lorraine Davis. She even had the name on her driver's license and all her credit cards changed. I guess the only reminder she wants of my dad, Dr. Robert Morgan, is me.

When we were a family of three we lived very differently than Mom and I do now. Ever since he left we've been pretty broke. Mom always had a job, even when she and my dad were still married. She worked for a law firm back then. Now she's an executive secretary for a large advertising agency on Madison Avenue.

Although Mom makes a pretty good salary, she still can't give me all the things that we could afford when my dad was around. I know it's rotten of me, but sometimes I get angry about our situation and take it out on Mom. Even though I understand she's doing her best, I lose total control every once in a while.

Mom put her hand on my arm. "You look better than good."

That was her way of apologizing.

"Now tell me," she said with a smile, "who's all this in honor of?"

"His name is Danny Booth." I looked at my mom. "He's the farrier's son." I waited for her to comment. She might have in the old days, but she just continued to smile and then asked how old he was, where I'd met him, what he did, where he lived . . . Mothers are so-o-o-o predictable.

Mom usually left the house before I did, but that morning I was just too hyper to sit around. By seven thirty I was on my way out the door.

"Julia, wait," Mom called from the kitchen. "How about some breakfast?"

"No, thanks, Mom." I couldn't believe she still nudged me like that. Here I was, a few months short of starting my freshman year at college, and she was still treating me like a little kid. "I'll grab a doughnut at Jake's."

"You call that breakfast?" she asked. "Come on, let me fix you something. It'll only take a minute."

"MOM!" I turned around, impatient to be off. "I'll be fine, honest!"

"Julia, honey. Hold on a minute."

"What? I gotta go." I was literally itching to get to the stable.

Mom got up and grabbed her purse from the shelf near the front door. "Do you have enough money for the shoeing?" she asked. Before I could answer she handed me five dollars.

"Just in case you need a little extra. Have a good day, honey." She gave me a kiss. "You sure you don't want to dry your hair before you leave?"

She always asks things like that instead of saying good-bye. I guess it's a mother thing.

"Yep, I'm positive. Uh, Mom . . . ?" She turned around.

"Yes, dear?"

"Thanks." I held up the five-dollar bill and smiled. "See you later." I quickly went out the door and started down the stairs.

I loved the noise my boots made on the steps as I clumped down the four flights of stairs to the lobby. Actually, it's not really a lobby. It's just a small entry hall inside of the double doors that lead to the street. Most of the tenants use the foyer to dump their junk mail before walking up to their apartments. Every time I walked through there and saw what a mess it was, I got really angry. It was kind of gross—not to mention embarrassing when I had friends over—living in such a dump.

We moved into this building the day after Mom found out about my dad's messing around. The divorce settlement didn't go too well for Mom; my dad got to keep the old apartment and our country house. Mom got a lot of the furniture, and most of the dishes and stuff. The only thing I'll miss about Mom's and my place when I'm up at school is the view. From the rooftop there is an absolutely spectacular panorama of Manhattan. I spend a lot of time up there. It's a great place to go to get away from things. Alone on the roof I didn't have to deal with anyone—I could sing to myself, daydream, or just think.

There is a big brick chimney in the middle of the roof. Sitting on one side of the chimney, I could look out over Central Park all the way to the gleaming white buildings of the Upper East Side. That was where most of my friends from Parkside lived. It's New York's fanciest neighborhood.

From the south side of the chimney, I could see midtown Manhattan. Midtown is amazing. It's mostly filled with giant glass skyscrapers. During the day the sun reflects so brightly off the office buildings that it can actually hurt your eyes. After dark, the lights inside the buildings seem to glow like stars.

From the north side the view isn't all that exciting. Our apartment is at the outer reaches of what is considered the "good part of the Upper West Side." A few blocks above us is Columbia University, and continuing north, Harlem. A lot of the buildings from this view are old and pretty run-down.

I only sat on the west side of the chimney once. It's not that the view isn't nice. Actually it's beautiful—almost like a postcard. From that vantage I could see all the way to the Hudson River and beyond to the shores of New Jersey. Unfortunately, right between our place and the river is this big, ritzy apartment building. And that's the problem. That beautiful building is where I used to live.

As if that weren't a depressing enough reminder of our recent drop down the social ladder! Not only could I see the building, I could see right into our old apartment. A really goofy guy with a crew cut has my room. He's got these posters of heavy-metal bands on the walls and junk thrown all over the floor, but it's still my old room. After seeing the disaster area, I figured why torture myself. I decided never to look back and forget about my dreams of what used to be and what might have been.

On my way to the stable, I stopped by

Jake's Donut Shop. I'd been going there almost every day since I started riding at Parkside. I even worked there after school for a while. It seems as though whenever I go into the little shop, the same customers are sitting on the same worn red vinyl stools sipping their coffee and eating doughnuts.

Jake saw me walk in and automatically fixed me a cup of coffee.

"Hey, little Julia, how 'ya doing?" Jake hollered as he wiped his hands off on his apron. "The usual?"

As I said, I've known Jake a very long time. When I was dealing with my parents' divorce, Jake was a really big help. "How about a cherry Danish? Maybe a nice glazed doughnut? They're still hot."

"No thanks, Jake," I said. "But I will take another coffee, please . . . to go. Oh, and I need some milk and sugar on the side, too, please."

"Sure, Julia. Who's it for?" Jake winked at me. "Say, do you got a new boyfriend?"

I must have turned bright red, because Jake started to laugh. So did the customers at the counter.

"So . . . that's the way it is, eh!" Jake said, still chuckling. He was always teasing me.

Still blushing, I paid for the coffee and turned to leave.

"See ya tomorrow," Jake called, as the door closed behind me. "Unless you run away and elope tonight."

"Well, that was totally humiliating. I can't believe he said that in front of everybody," I muttered to myself as I walked across Eighty-ninth Street toward Parkside. "What's so funny about my having a boyfriend, anyway. Besides, it's not as if he *were* my boyfriend or anything. Sure, he's a boy . . . and I'd like us to be friends, but . . ."

Suddenly a hand grabbed my arm and spun me around. *"Julia!"* It was Susan, and she had this big grin spread across her face. "You were talking to yourself like a bag lady." She dropped into step alongside me. "What's your problem? Hey, new britches? Gonna get Mirage shod? Is that coffee you got there?"

Susan has this incredibly annoying habit of asking a ton of questions right in a row without giving you time to answer any of them.

"Nothing! . . . Yes! . . . Yes! . . . Yes, two! . . . So?"

"No biggie." Susan shrugged. "Do you have a coffee in there for me? Your best friend?"

"Nope." I shook my head. "One for me and one for . . ." I faltered for a minute.

"For Danny, right? Well, well. It really is serious!" Susan pounced on the information.

I drew myself up to my full five feet two inches. "Susan, please grow up!" I said. I was trying to act mature and pretend that I wasn't nervous. As we crossed the street, Danny's truck pulled up, and I immediately felt my heart begin to pound loudly in my chest. In fact, I bet everyone in Manhattan heard it thumping away. I tried to calm myself down by taking some deep breaths.

"Do I look okay?" I asked Susan.

"Marvelous, dahling. Simply mah-vul-ous!" Susan grinned but stopped when she saw the stern look on my face. "Seriously, Julia," she added in her normal voice—she knew that this guy stuff was new to me—"you look great. Danny is going to think you're hot. Listen, I gotta go. 'Bye." She ran off, skipping toward the stables.

I walked slowly over to the truck, where Danny was unloading equipment. Normally I don't have heart palpitations when I see a guy, and I could usually manage to say something fairly normal. But that morning I could barely squeak out a "Hello."

It was bizarre. When I didn't care about a guy, I could joke around and think of witty things to say with no problem. But the minute that I was at all interested in someone, I was completely tongue-tied.

Danny looked up and smiled at me. He had an amazing smile that caused a warm glow in the pit of my stomach and spread throughout my body.

"Hi," Danny said, continuing to unload his tools. Maybe it was just a little early in the day for a big conversation, I thought, hoping my totally irrational disappointment didn't show.

"I brought us some coffee," I said, holding out the bag. "I wasn't sure how you took yours, so I got milk and sugar on the side." I suddenly felt like a waitress in a diner.

"Uh, thanks."

He took the coffee from my hands. I guess the bottom of the bag had gotten wet, because when he grabbed the top of it, the cups fell through the paper and went crashing onto the pavement. I jumped back so that my britches wouldn't get ruined; Danny got covered with coffee.

"Oh, my gosh," I cried. "I'm so sorry."

Danny glanced down at his coffee-stained jeans and then up at me. We both started to laugh.

"Well," he said, "coffee usually has more of an effect on me when I drink it. But who knows? This may work out just fine. I suppose I'll absorb some caffeine through my jeans!"

I started to wipe his leg with a napkin, but Danny shook his head and said, "It's okay. Don't worry about it. They needed a washing anyway."

Jake had put two doughnuts in the bag without my noticing. Luckily, they were still wrapped in those little wax-paper sacks, so they didn't get soaked. We sat on the low wall outside of Parkside, munching on our slightly soggy doughnuts as we stared at the river of coffee that trickled through the cracks in the sidewalk.

Danny finished his doughnut first and, after licking his fingers clean, suggested that I go get Mirage while he got us a couple of cups of fresh coffee from the vending machine inside the stable office.

"That is," he added, "if you still trust me with hot liquid."

"Sure," I joked. "After all, you're the one wearing the last two cups—not me."

I jumped up and ran into the cool darkness of the stable. One thing I had learned from watching old comedies on the Late Show is always to leave on a good exit line.

I took the ramp up to Mirage's stall at a dead run. When I got to the top, I let out a low whistle, then another. Mirage whinnied his greeting in return. I kept whistling and he kept whinnying until I reached him. We did this every morning. It was noisy, but I loved it and so did Mirage.

I clambered under the chain that

stretched across the entrance to his stall and put my arms around his neck. We indulged in a mutual nuzzle for a minute before he pulled away, impatient for his morning apple.

Horses are the world's messiest eaters. You feed a horse a snack by putting your hand out—palm up and fingers together —with the food in the middle. You keep your fingers together so that the horse doesn't bite you. Although horses are not generally biters, a finger can look and feel dangerously similar to a carrot.

Mirage sucked the entire apple into his mouth and proceeded to chomp hungrily. He kept dropping chunks of half-chewed apple mixed with his foamy, white saliva onto my hand. I know that sounds disgusting, but I guess the way I felt about Mirage is the way mothers feel about their babies. Even the gross things they do are cute.

Mindful of the fact that my new britches had already escaped one big mess that morning, rather than smearing mushed apple on my pants leg, I wiped my hand on the towel I kept hanging in the stall.

An old camp trunk filled with my grooming brushes stood right outside of Mirage's stall. I unlocked it—the combination was the date when I got Mirage—took out the currying brushes and combs, and got to work getting Mirage cleaned up.

"Who's a good horse?" I crooned. "Who's Mommy's baby?" I always kept up a running monologue as I groomed him. "We're going to get you new shoes today, aren't we? You have to look all pretty for Uncle Danny. Yes, you do."

"Uncle Danny?" It was Susan.

I jumped. Susan had crept into Mirage's stall without my hearing. This was another habit of hers—sneaking up on you.

"You're really losing it," she said, slowly shaking her head from side to side.

"What?" I asked. "I just wanted Mirage to know what was going on." My excuse sounded lame, even to me.

Susan just snorted. "Well, Uncle Danny is waiting downstairs with two coffees. What did you do, pour the last cups on him? Smooth move." She giggled and ducked into one of the other stalls.

"I don't have time to deal with you now, Susan. But you'd better start sleeping with one eye open." I tried to sound as menacing as possible.

"Come on, Mirage." I slipped Mirage's halter over his head, snapped on the lead chain, and led him into the aisle separating the stalls. He followed me to the ramp and out to where Danny was waiting with the coffee. Mirage never forgets a friend. When he saw Danny, he let out a snort and trotted right over to him.

"Mirage, no!" I yelled, but I was wasting my breath. Mirage had raced up to Danny and butted him with his head. For the second time that morning, Danny was wearing our coffee.

I couldn't help laughing. He looked ridiculous standing there holding the two empty Styrofoam cups with coffee slowly spreading down the front of his jeans.

"What's so funny?" He was obviously less than amused.

"I've heard of trial by fire," I answered, "but *never* trial by caffeine."

56

Fortunately, Danny had a sense of humor. He gave me a stern look before cracking up. With a wide grin on his face, he tossed the empty cups into the garbage bin. "Maybe we'd better just concentrate on Mirage's shoes and skip the coffee," he said.

Danny reached into the back of his truck and took out the heavy leather apron that farriers wear when they work. He slipped it over his head and tied the string behind his back.

"Maybe you should consider wearing that the next time we have coffee."

"I'll consider it," Danny joked. Then he tied Mirage to one of the rings welded to the side of the truck and lifted Mirage's left front hoof onto his lap.

A lot of owners leave their horses with the farrier and go about their business until the horse is done. But even when Mr. Booth was shoeing Mirage, I always stuck around to watch. Now, however, with Danny doing the shoeing, a sale at Bloomingdale's and a charge card with unlimited credit couldn't have torn me away. Well, at least maybe not right away.

Shoeing a horse is a three-step project. The first step is to remove the old shoe. The farrier pries it off and removes any nails with a claw hammer. Then he files and trims down the hoof, which is like a big, thick toenail.

The second step is heating and shaping the new shoe on the anvil that farriers keep in the back of their trucks. They heat the shoe until it's white hot and then use a very heavy hammer to make the shoe fit the hoof perfectly. It's hard work, but it's all necessary to ensure that your horse doesn't come up lame. That's why most farriers are well paid—and well built.

The final step is putting the shoe back on the horse. The shoe is still hot from the forge when it's attached to the horse by nails that are driven into the base of the hoof. I know it sounds painful, but if it's done properly it doesn't hurt the horse any more than a pedicure hurts a person.

I usually allowed Mirage to rest in his stall for a few hours after he got shod. So, when Danny was finished, I led my horse back upstairs and gave him a little extra alfalfa.

I left the stable and walked back to Jake's Donut Shop. I returned in a few minutes with two more coffees and Jake's laughter ringing in my ears. How he knew about the spilled coffee was beyond me.

Danny must have stepped away for a minute, so I set his coffee down and went upstairs to drink mine with Mirage. I figured Danny had shown unusually good humor so far today, but three spills in just one morning would have really been pushing my luck.

CHAPTER

FOUR

One of the things I love most about living in New York is the way the old and the new coexist. Right next to modern-day architectural wonders are buildings that were built in the 1800s. You can find a CD store in the same building as a bodega—a Spanish grocery store—that has been in the same family for three generations. Huge buses run right alongside horse-drawn carriages.

Parkside Stables is over a hundred years old. It was originally a carriage house where wealthy families kept their teams of horses and carriages. As cars took over the streets, Parkside became a riding stable. Now, it's the only riding academy in all of Manhattan.

Parkside's annual winter and summer horse shows were the high points of my year. I loved showing Mirage. The fact that Danny would probably be there on the day of this year's summer show didn't exactly *dim* my excitement level either!

On the day of the show, I ran all the way to Parkside and practically flew up the steps which led into the stable office.

It was still hours before the show began, but the tension level was already starting to build. The hackers, which is how we owners refer to the people who come to take lessons on the rental horses, were starting to collect at the desk. Everybody has a favorite horse to ride, and they were busy trying to make sure they got the mount they wanted to show on. Peter Gordon was trying to deal with everything.

Peter's family had owned Parkside for three generations. He often said he liked horses better than most people. Come to think of it, so did I.

I hadn't always felt that way—about people, I mean. When I was younger I had lots of friends, and I wasn't shy at all. Then my dad left, and it suddenly got harder for me to make friends. I guess the divorce really changed me. Now I just don't seem to want to get close to people.

Anyway, Peter was behind the desk trying to make everybody happy. I waved to him as I pushed my way through the crowd. He looked up at me and rolled his eyes. I knew he was having one of those days. I threw him a salute and ran up the ramp to see Mirage.

Susan was already there and had started grooming him. She'd given him his bath and had finished wiping him down in preparation for the show.

Grooming a horse properly requires hours of work. Susan had already rubbed Mirage down and curried and brushed him. I picked up a comb and began to braid his mane, while she started braiding his tail.

I looped a bunch of rubber bands over my wrist so that they would be easily accessible. "So where do you think Denise, Laura, and Penny are?" I asked Susan.

Susan began talking in a falsetto as she continued to work on Mirage. "Oh, Susan, dear," she said, imitating Laura perfectly. "We're going to Millers to buy some accessories. Would you care to join us."

I was laughing so hard that I dropped Mirage's mane, and all my braiding unraveled. When Susan saw this she began laughing, too.

Millers was the most expensive place in the city to buy riding equipment. It was typical of Laura to spend the morning of a show shopping instead of grooming. It was also very "Laura" to invite Susan to tag along. Laura knew that Susan couldn't afford to shop at Millers. For that matter, neither could I.

"I bet she hired one of the grooms to get Money ready," I said.

Susan shook her head. "Nope!" She pulled a beautiful set of red leg wraps out of Mirage's tack box. "I traded her," she said, grinning. "One set of hardly-ever-been-used leg wraps in exchange for one beautifully groomed horse!"

We high-fived. The leg wraps were exactly what Mirage needed for the show.

"When are you going to get Money ready?" I asked her.

"Well, I got here early, so I figure we'll be done in another hour. That will leave me a couple of hours before the dressage class at one. It won't take me more than a half hour to tack Money up for Laura's jump class at three."

I was entering the same class as Laura, but Mirage would already be tacked up from Susan's class.

The show was a combined training show. That means both dressage, which is like horse dancing, and jumping, which is when the horse is ridden over series of fences, will take place.

I knew Susan was going to do well in the dressage class. She and Mirage were wonderful at that. I didn't care if I won the jump class, I just wanted to beat Laura and Denise. That would take the wind out of their sails.

Mirage was much smaller than the other girls' horses: a severe disadvantage when you're asking a horse to clear a high fence. But it didn't matter how short or tall Mirage was; he had a lot of heart. He would do anything for me. And I for him.

A lot of girls who own horses lose interest when they reach the age of thirteen or fourteen and discover boys. That never happened to me. It's not that I'm not as crazy about guys as everyone else; it's just that for a long time I was even crazier about Mirage.

When Susan and I had finished braiding Mirage, she left to work on Money. I was rubbing saddle oil into Mirage's tack when the girls returned from their shopping expedition. Laura had so many bags that she had to ask two of the grooms to help her carry them up the ramp to the stalls.

"Look, my new colors," she said, dumping out a new saddle pad, leg wraps, nose band, helmet cover, and a bunch of other stuff onto the floor of the stall.

You can choose your own horse's colors. Usually you try to have all the bits and pieces match. Laura used to show with red colors, but all her new stuff was

66

bright purple. That explained her trading sixty dollars' worth of leg wraps to Susan.

"Wow! Really nice," I said, as I rubbed even harder. Her new stuff looked great. I had to admit I was envious.

"You can use my old red saddle pad if you want," Laura said.

I looked up, surprised at her generous offer. "Thanks," I said, smiling. Sometimes, in spite of being a major snob, Laura could be very nice.

She turned and started walking out of Mirage's stall. "Susan!" she hollered as she walked down the aisle. "Is my Money ready yet?"

Then again, sometimes Laura could be a real pain in the you-know-what. Still, never one to look a gift saddle pad in the mouth, I went and got it from her tack box.

After I put the saddle pad and saddle on Mirage I stepped back to admire him. I had to admit, Mirage looked incredibly handsome in red. It was a big relief to be able to immerse myself in Mirage. At that moment I wasn't thinking about my dad, the upcoming school year, Mom's money problems, or even Danny. My total focus was on my wonderful horse. He was the one thing in my life that I had no doubts about, no fears—only good feelings.

I finished getting Mirage ready for the show. As I gave him a quick once-over, a lump came to my throat. His saddle and bridle were a beautiful black leather. The contrast of the black leather, red leg wraps and saddle pad, and his gleaming white coat was breathtaking. I found some red ribbon and tied little red bows at the bottom of each braid. It was perfect.

Susan came back into the stall and, in a voice just barely audible, whispered, "Wow, he's beautiful."

I was so happy and proud.

The loudspeaker interrupted my reverie. "One half hour to the first dressage event, ladies and gentlemen. Riders, attend to your mounts."

"OHMYGOSH!" I shouted. Susan and I started jumping up and down. "Here, put on my jacket. I want to see what's going on in the arena," I said.

Susan grabbed my old show jacket off

the hanger as I ran halfway down the ramp. I leaned over the banister and looked down into the ring.

They'd done a fantastic job cleaning Parkside up for the show. There was a fresh coat of whitewash on the century-old wood walls, and the arena had been freshly raked.

Spectators packed the arena. Metal folding chairs had been set up along the edge of the ring, as many as four deep in the corners. I always loved watching the people who didn't ride and who were only there because a family member had made them come. They tiptoed around, holding up their pants so that the bottoms wouldn't get dirty. They gingerly picked their way through the combination of dirt and horse dung that made up the arena floor. And they turned up their noses at all the horse smells. It cracked me up. These people spent every day in New York City, the dirtiest, smelliest city in America. Still they fell apart completely when they were exposed to a little taste of old-fashioned country living.

"Can you believe the stench in here?"

I overheard one heavily jeweled lady say to her companion as she sniffed the air.

Mom had said that she would come and watch me ride if she could get away from the office. I looked around the arena and saw her entering through the ramp that led to Eighty-ninth Street. I was really proud of her. She looked young and pretty, and unlike a lot of the parents, she looked right at home in the stable. She should; she'd been coming to horse shows since I was a little kid.

Mom found a seat near the edge of the ring. It wasn't exactly front row center where I would have chosen for her to sit, but I guess it was okay. However, on the other side of the arena there was an empty seat next to a good-looking dad who I happened to know was divorced. Now that was a much better seat.

Since my dad left, Mom had gone out with maybe three guys, and none of them had lasted more than two or three dates. It's as if the experience with my dad had soured her on men in general. It's not that she doesn't like them, it's just that I don't think she trusts them anymore. And, unfortunately, I had let her fears and feelings become my own. Not that I didn't want a boyfriend, it's just that I was afraid that as soon as I started to like someone, he'd turn around and dump me.

When you're a kid, you tend to think your parents are always right. I guess I'd picked up Mom's distrust of men and had integrated it into my own life. It's funny, but just as I had to learn that my friends' opinions weren't always right, I had to learn to reject some of Mom's opinions. If I didn't distance myself from Mom's pain, I'd never have any experiences of my own. I already knew what it felt like to be hurt. Now I was ready for some happiness.

I waved to Mom from the ramp, but she didn't see me, so I ran down into the arena to give her a hug.

"Julia! You look terrific." As soon as this was out of her mouth, she stood up and began to adjust my stock tie. Typical Mom!

I quickly moved out of reach before she had a chance to lick her fingers and slick down my curls. Mothers, what are you going to do with them?

"Come on, Mom," I said, putting my tie back the way it had been. "I'm fine. Anyhow, I'm glad you made it here. Uh . . . are you sure you want to sit way over here?"

Mom looked at her seat and then around the arena. "Yes. Why? I can see perfectly well."

I tried again. "Don't you want to sit over there? How about that seat?" I pointed to the vacant seat across the arena next to the single dad.

I grabbed her purse and started to walk toward the seat that I had selected for her. Before I could take even two steps in what I considered the right direction, Mom grabbed my arm.

"Stop trying to play matchmaker, Julia," she ordered. "I came to see you ride, not be a participant in Parkside's version of *Love Connection*!"

I'm a bit ashamed now when I think back on my eagerness to get Mom hooked up with someone. I guess I didn't fully understand what she was going through. She still had a lot to work out on her own before she was ready to involve someone else.

"Oh, Mom!" I said, rolling my eyes.

Mom and I, as was usual when we got on the subject of her dating, had reached an impasse.

"Okay, have it your way." I shrugged. "Well, I have to go back upstairs and help Susan get Mirage ready."

I leaned down to give her a kiss on the cheek, then ran back up the aisle to Mirage's stall.

At the top of the ramp I stopped and looked back into the arena. I was hoping to see Danny. This would be a perfect time to introduce him to Mom. The idea made me a little nervous. I had never brought a guy home to meet my mother before, but something told me Danny was going to be different from the rest.

I don't know why I felt that way. Maybe it was the tingly sensation I got whenever he was around. I'd never been so excited about seeing a guy before. But I couldn't stop myself from wanting to see Danny. There was something about him that made me lose control and live in the moment.

Danny wasn't in the ring yet. I hoped

that he was just running a little late. After all, he hadn't promised to come.

"JULIA!" Susan's stage whisper could have been heard all the way to California. "COME HERE!" I sprinted up to Mirage's stall.

The toughest part about getting ready for a show has nothing to do with the horse. It's the tying of the stock tie—an extremely complicated, ornamental tie worn by the riders.

By the time I got to the stall Susan had this desperate look in her eyes. "I can't do it. I absolutely cannot tie this thing!"

She looked as if she was about to cry. I stood behind her and reached my arms around her neck.

"Like this," I said, tying it for her. It's always easier to do it on someone else. "Okay, turn around," I ordered.

Susan faced me, and I made a few minor adjustments to her outfit. I helped her straighten the lapels of the show jacket and centered her tie.

"You ready?" I asked. She nodded without speaking. She was obviously very nervous. "Smile, silly. You know you're the best rider in the class. Anyhow, Mirage will take care of *you.*" Susan managed a weak smile as I turned away.

"Hey, wait a minute," she said. "I'll take care of *him.* I'm the one who's been working on his training for the last six months."

I turned around, smiling. "So?" I asked. "What's the panic? You'll do great!" I gave her a hug, and we walked Mirage over to the top of the ramp.

Peter was standing in the center of the arena, finishing his welcoming remarks. "And so, ladies and gentlemen, it is with great pride that I welcome you to this, our Tenth Annual Summer Horse Show. Would the first dressage class please assemble in the arena."

Susan and I looked at each other. "Thanks for calming me down," she said with a smile.

"What are friends for?" I answered.

She gave me a "thumbs up" and I returned the gesture as I said "Good luck." Then I stood there watching as my two best friends—Mirage and Susan—headed down the ramp.

The term "dressage" comes from the

French verb *dresser*, which, when applied to horses, means training. Surprisingly, though, it was the Spanish who first used dressage to train their cavalry horses. The training provided especially good conditioning and made the horses particularly obedient.

The objective of dressage competition is to make the horse and rider appear to move as one. The horse is supposed to be "on the bit," which means moving forward into the bit—the piece of metal that goes in his mouth. When the rider applies leg pressure or shifts weight balance, the horse does complicated movements like crossing its legs at the trot or moving sideways while cantering. It's hard to explain but beautiful to watch.

Arabian horses, like Mirage, have fewer vertebrae in their necks, backs, and tails than Thoroughbreds. Since their frame is shorter and less flexible, it's harder for them to do the difficult movements. Somehow, Mirage always made it look easy. Okay, so maybe Susan had something to do with it, too.

When I heard Peter's announcement, my heart started to pound in my chest.

"Next up, Susan Goodman riding Mirage, owned by Julia Morgan."

I held my breath as Susan walked Mirage into the ring. She stopped in the center, dropped her right arm, and bowed her head. That's the way you have to start each dressage performance. Then Susan and Mirage began the movements for the first-level test. I knew I was mumbling under my breath, "Trot to the right, twenty-meter circle, change diagonal in the half school, trot left, canter across the ring," as I watched the performance. They were absolutely perfect. Mirage was completely obedient, which is the main thing that the judge is looking for. Susan's position was flawless—you couldn't see her give the commands at all.

They came to a halt in the center, Susan bowed, and they walked on a loose rein out of the ring.

I could barely stand still while I watched the last contestant perform, but finally it was over. My fingers were crossed as I waited for the judge to announce the results. When he did, I clapped my hands and jumped up and down. Susan and Mirage had won first place.

I don't think I have ever been as proud in my life as when the judge pinned the blue ribbon on Mirage's bridle and Peter announced, "First place to Susan Goodman, riding Mirage, owned by Julia Morgan."

One thing I know for certain—although I've had some good days since then, and I have faith that even better days are yet to come—I haven't had the same kind of innocent happiness *since* that moment.

After the ribbons were presented, I ran down into the ring and over to Susan. "You did it! You did it!" I said in a stage whisper as I grabbed on to Mirage's rein while Susan dismounted. Susan tried to act very nonchalant about her victory, but the ear-to-ear grin that spread across her face was a dead giveaway.

Mom hopped out of her seat and came over to give Susan a big hug. Susan and Mom get along really well. In fact, they did better together than Mom and I did most of the time. Maybe that's because Susan is a few years younger than I am and doesn't mind the excessive mothering.

While Mom congratulated Susan, I pulled Mirage's reins over his head so that I could use them as a lead rein. Susan gave me a high-five and then hugged Mirage's neck. She turned back to me and said, "Gotta get ready for the next one." Then she turned and ran upstairs to tack up Money for Laura.

Mom returned to the stands and I walked Mirage out into the street to cool him off. Danny was in the driveway leaning against the side of his truck. He'd been watching the class through the open doorway.

"Congratulations," he said, giving me a big smile.

"It's really Susan and Mirage that deserve it, but thanks." I wasn't sure what to say next, so I just started stroking Mirage's neck.

"So, are you going to show him, too?"

I nodded. Danny shrugged.

"Dumb question," he said sheepishly. "Why else would you be all dressed up?"

I was happy to have Danny there, but once again I found myself tongue-tied.

With Mom, Susan, and Danny, I felt that I had my own personal cheering section. For the first time in the past two years, I was part of something.

Looking back on it, I guess that my feeling of isolation was pretty much my own fault. Mom and I basically cut off all our old friends when my dad left. For Mom I think it was plain embarrassment over our reduced circumstances. For me, well, I cut my friends off because I thought that they'd eventually cut me off and I didn't want them to do it first. I know I probably should have had more faith in them, but I had had total faith in my dad, and he left us without even a backward glance.

After my dad left I expected him to call me all the time, but he didn't. I thought that because he was such a wonderful person, it had to have been my fault that he wasn't calling. It must have been because I was a terrible person or something. I know better now, but for a long time I just couldn't understand what was really happening to my family. Rather than risk that kind of rejection again, I did the rejecting. Either way, I ended up pretty much alone.

Having Danny come to the show to watch me felt, well, it felt great! It was the first time I wanted to open up to anybody, especially a boy, since the divorce. It wasn't really fair of me—after not expecting anything from anyone for so long, I expected too much from Danny, too fast. I guess I hoped he would be some sort of "all-knowing/all-understanding guy," the way I used to think of my dad. And that's too much to expect from anyone. Danny was great, but he wasn't perfect.

Danny walked over to Mirage and looked him over. He rested his hand on the red saddle pad. "Nice tack," he said. "I suppose you went out and bought some new stuff for the show?"

For some reason I let his comment really spoil my mood. "You really have an attitude, and I'm getting tired of it," I screamed at him. "I'm not a spoiled rich kid. Everyone else can remember that, why can't you?"

I had wanted so badly for him to be there to see me show, and I had been eager to introduce him to Mom, but at that moment I didn't even want to be near him. Looking back on it I think that I was so happy to see him that I scared myself. I reverted to my natural instincts, and rejected him before he could reject me.

Danny just stood there, shocked, as I turned on my heel, gave Mirage's bridle a tug, and headed back inside. We returned to the arena and waited for the instructors to finish setting up for the jump class.

Show jumping is really different from dressage. In dressage the rider sits very erect, whereas in jumping the rider takes what is known as the "forward seat." The stirrups are much shorter for jumping; that way the rider can get off the horse's back. This makes it much easier for the horse to lift both its weight, and the rider's, over the fence.

Fences are placed throughout the arena and are adjusted for height and width. The Parkside arena is fairly small with low ceilings, so none of the fences was over five feet high or over two and a half feet wide. Still, the course that the instructors had set up looked pretty tough.

I mounted Mirage as the other entrants came into the ring. Mirage and I walked the course, and I let him sniff and look at all the fences. That way, when we cantered over to them, he wouldn't be afraid. It helped me get back my focus, too. If I wanted to win I had to stop thinking about Danny. Knowing how I'd just treated him, I was having a hard time concentrating totally on the course.

A few minutes after I'd entered the ring, Susan joined me. She took off my show jacket and helped me into it. Then she held out a piece of sugar for Mirage and gave me a good-luck hug. "Let's make it two for two," she urged.

"We'll try," I said, as I got up into the saddle. I looked down at Susan and gave her the "thumbs up," which she returned with a laugh.

Before jumping a horse over fences, it's a good idea to warm him up by trotting around the arena for a few minutes. Susan had already ridden Mirage, but almost a half hour had passed, so I wanted to take him around the ring at a trot a couple of times.

I had always taken good care of Mirage; since my parents' breakup, I'd been fanatical about it. Outside of school, which Mom *made* me take seriously, Mirage had become my whole life.

We'd gone about fifteen feet when I felt Mirage suddenly shudder and then begin to limp. I didn't know what was happening. My heart literally stopped beating, and I felt myself break out in a cold sweat. I could feel myself beginning to panic. What was wrong with him?

I trotted him a few more strides just to make sure I hadn't imagined the limp. There was no question about it. He was definitely lame and favoring his left front leg. I couldn't show him without causing him pain and possibly creating a more serious injury.

I'm still embarrassed when I think back to the way I reacted. As I started out of the arena, I began to shake and sob uncontrollably. I wasn't crying for Mirage; I was crying for myself. He was the only thing in my life that had never let me down. With Mirage going lame, I couldn't trust anything to stay good in my life.

I quickly dismounted, loosened Mirage's girth, and led him back up the ramp to his stall. I was still crying as I untacked him, but by then I was also feeling bad for him.

"Julia!" Mom came running into the stall out of breath. "What's wrong with Mirage?"

"I don't know, Mom," I cried. "I don't know!" When she tried to put her arm around me, I shrugged it off. "Just go back to work. I'm not going to be showing him now."

I know it was kind of cold of me to act that way, but I was so scared about Mirage that I couldn't stand the idea of having anyone around. Particularly Mom. There's nothing worse when you are trying not to cry than having your mother hug you. It's almost a guarantee for tears.

Mom looked at me for a minute. "Okay," she said, backing away a little. I could tell by the sound of her voice that her feelings were hurt. "I'll see you at home, then."

I know I should have been nicer to

Mom, but Mirage was mine and I sort of felt that if I let anyone else get involved with him maybe they'd take him away.

Susan was the only person I even let ride him. If I hadn't known I was going to have to give him up in the fall, I don't think I would have let her get as close to him as I did. It doesn't make a lot of sense if you think about it, but it *felt* as if it did at the time.

I took off Mirage's leg wraps, the wraps that were supposed to protect his shins and ankles. There was a small swelling under his left front leg wrap at the knee joint. I couldn't believe that it had been there when I got him tacked up. There was no way I would have just missed it. I figured it must have happened during the show.

As I undid the rest of the leg wraps, I tried to stay calm. I had him almost totally untacked when Susan came flying into his stall.

"What happened?" she asked, panting. "I was getting Laura up on Money and didn't see you leave. Is everything okay?"

I turned to face her and started to cry. I

can't believe how mean and childish I acted toward Susan. She was only trying to help, but when I used to be upset I didn't want to have someone to talk to, I just wanted to have someone to blame. Just as I did when my dad left.

"No! Everything's not okay! What did you do to him?" I was sobbing and my breath was ragged. "He was fine until you rode him. I trusted you! Look what you did!" I shouted, pointing to the swelling on his leg.

Susan tried to speak, but I cut her off.

"He must have overreached when you had him doing those fancy dressage movements. He must have kicked himself because he wasn't ready to perform all those stupid tricks! You did this to Mirage!"

Susan was shocked. "Julia, I'm sorry. But I didn't do anything. Honest!" she argued. "You saw. You were there. Mirage was perfectly fine when I finished. How could you say that? You can't possibly believe I'd do anything to hurt Mirage. I love him, too." Susan bent down and ran her hand over the lump.

"Right," I yelled. "That's why he came

up lame, because you didn't do anything! Maybe you didn't warm him up enough before you rode. Maybe you're not as good as you think you are. You don't know everything, you know." I was crying so hard that I had begun to hiccup.

"How can you think that?" By now Susan was crying, too. "I'd never, ever hurt him." She stood up and wrapped her arms around Mirage's neck.

Mirage was ignoring both of us. He stood there calmly munching the carrots I'd gotten him for a post-show treat.

"Please," Susan begged. "What can I do?"

"Just leave us alone!" I screamed at her. "Get out of here. Stay away from me and my horse!"

Susan stood still for a moment before she turned and ran out of the stall crying hysterically. I could hear her footsteps and sobs fade in the distance as she went down the ramp.

CHAPTER

FIVE

I had almost stopped crying when Danny came up behind me.

"Hey. Are you okay?" he asked, putting his hand on my shoulder.

I sniffled a bit and rubbed my eyes with the back of my hand. Trying to smile, I asked him, "Do I have any mascara left on at all?"

"Uh, yeah. I guess so, but it's mostly on your cheeks, not your eyelashes." He reached out and gently wiped my face. "Why are you crying? I thought Mirage took a blue ribbon in the dressage test.

Didn't you guys place in the jump class?"

Before I could answer, he continued. "Listen," he said. "I'm sorry I was such a —well, I'm sorry I didn't come in to see you ride. I just wanted to cool off. I hope you're not mad."

"It's not that at all." Conscious of my puffy eyes I turned away, picked up a curry comb, and started to groom Mirage. "Mirage went lame before the class." I could feel the sobs building in my chest. "I got so scared. I love him so much. I didn't know what I'd do if anything were seriously wrong with him."

I didn't want Danny to see me cry. I wasn't even sure if I wanted him to be there at that moment, but he didn't offer me too much choice.

Danny put his hands on my shoulders and turned me around. "You've come to the right guy," he said, spreading his hands expansively. "Danny Booth. V.I.T. That's Vet in Training. At your service!"

I must have looked doubtful, because he added, "And a farrier to boot. Out of that stall," he ordered. "Let an expert take a look."

I could hear the applause of the crowd downstairs as I moved away from Mirage. Danny stepped into the stall and ran a firm hand down Mirage's neck.

It's always a good idea when approaching a horse to put your hand on him. This way he knows that you're not going to hurt him.

"Okay," Danny said, turning around to face me. "Do you know which leg is off?"

"Left front—at the knee. There's a lump."

Danny gently stroked Mirage's left haunch. He reached down and lifted up the hoof. "Do you have a hoof pick handy?"

I reached for my grooming box and searched through it before I pulled out a hoof pick. It's a small hook-shaped tool used to clean rocks or mud out of a horse's hoof.

"Here it is," I said. My hands were shaking as I gave it to him. For an instant our eyes locked, and I could see a warmth and compassion in Danny's that I hadn't noticed before. It was very comforting; it made me trust him.

Another wave of applause, even louder than the first, rose from the arena. I should have been down there on Mirage receiving the crowd's adulation instead of up here bawling my eyes out. It was so ironic. The people in the stands sounded so happy, while I felt as if my world was falling apart. Tears welled up in my eyes again, but I blinked them back. It was weird enough letting Danny see me cry; I didn't want him to see me lose it entirely.

In spite of my efforts, he knew I was extremely upset. He put his hand on my shoulder and whispered, "Hey, don't worry. I'm sure it's nothing serious. Now go sit down in the corner and let me check out my patient."

Danny carefully cleaned out the hoof. Then, tucking the pick in his back pocket he probed the frog—the inside front part of the hoof. The frog is kind of like the palm of a person's hand. I watched Danny as he worked. His hands were steady and gentle, and his eyes were bright and determined.

"Okay, the hoof is solid," he said, running his hand down Mirage's left front leg. When he touched the knee joint, Mirage shifted his weight. Danny had obviously felt the lump, too.

"There is something under the skin," he said quietly. "It's probably nothing serious."

Danny looked at me and gave me a reassuring smile. Then he went around to Mirage's right hindquarter to clean and probe that hoof. I could tell by the calming way he was handling Mirage—and me—that he was going to be a great vet.

"Tell you what, Julia," he suggested. "Why don't you trot Mirage up and down the aisle, and we'll see how he looks? Okay?"

Silently, I snapped on Mirage's halter and lead rope. Then I led him out of his stall. Danny leaned against the edge of the stall and watched as I coaxed Mirage into a trot.

"Okay," Danny said, joining me at the end of the aisle. "Trot him back to the stall."

I signaled Mirage, and we trotted slowly back to the stall.

"You're right," he said when we got there. "It's definitely the left front."

"Danny, I *know* that, but I still don't know what's causing the lump. Did he kick himself? Is it a strained ligament? Is it a muscle pull?" I leaned against Mirage's back. "Tell me that he's going to be all right," I pleaded. "Please?"

Danny looked at me for a moment and then seemed to brighten up. He cleared his throat, and in a comical German accent said, "Vell, de technical name for vats wrong mit him is complicated, but if you vant my expert diagnozees, it's called a 'boo-boo'!"

I couldn't believe him. I looked at Danny for an instant and then burst out laughing. He had managed to divert my attention from Mirage. Immediately I felt better. "A 'boo-boo'? That's what it's called?"

Danny smiled at me and said, "See, the patient has improved already. I am one incredible doctor. You should see my bedside manner," he added mischievously.

"I'll stick to 'stall-side' manners for now, thank you. Anyway," I protested, "I'm not the patient."

"Well," he conceded, "that may be so,

but Mirage wasn't crying when I came up here. You were."

Then Danny became serious again. "Look, it's probably just a sore muscle. Tell you what, let me ask my dad to stop by and check out Mirage when he gets a chance. Okay? Then, if he can't fix it because it's something more serious, we could call a vet. Okay?"

I shook my head. I was calm enough to realize that horses do come up lame sometimes, and it would have been totally overreacting to call in the vet until I'd tried a few home remedies myself.

"Isn't there anything I can do for him now?" I asked.

Danny stroked his chin seriously for a moment and then said, "Well, there is one thing."

"What?" I asked eagerly.

"I know Mirage would feel much better if *we* got a cup of coffee." Mirage chose that particular moment to kick over his water bucket.

Danny grinned and said, "See, he agrees! Of course, we'll try something unique this time, like drinking our coffee instead of wearing it. Okay?"

"Okay. I mean, who am I to argue with my horse?" I said with a smile. I wasn't totally comfortable with the idea. Part of me wanted to stay with Mirage, but there was this other part urging me to go.

I refilled the water bucket and mucked out the soggy hay from the stall, while Danny went down to the arena to find his dad and ask him to check on Mirage.

When I'd cleaned up the stall, I headed down the ramp and out into the sunlight. As the final burst of applause erupted, Danny exited the arena.

"I couldn't find my dad," he said. "I'll talk to him later, though. Come on." Danny held out his hand to me. "Let's fight through the crowd and get that cup of medicinal coffee."

I nodded, and we more or less patiently made our way onto the street.

The show had just finished, and large groups of participants and their supporters had begun to gather outside the stable on Eighty-ninth Street. Denise and Penny were there with Laura, who had a blue ribbon pinned on her jacket.

Danny and I walked over to congratulate her, but she was too busy accepting kudos from her parents and all her blue-blooded friends to take much notice of us. Danny was still holding my hand, and he pulled me on down Eighty-ninth Street toward Jake's.

By the time we got to Jake's, there wasn't an empty seat in the place. I'd never seen the doughnut shop so busy; it was twice as packed as the morning rush. It looked as if everyone who rode, had ever ridden, or ever would ride had come into Jake's. And this was in addition to Jake's regular clientele. The contrast was hilarious—riding britches and hard hats side by side, sipping coffee out of stained, cracked, and chipped mugs. What a city!

Danny and I took one look at the crowd and mutually decided to get take-out. We wanted to find a nice quiet place to sit on the street and talk. Jake saw me elbowing my way up to the counter and had my coffee ready for me when I got there. Danny ordered his coffee, and Jake quickly poured him a steaming cup.

I had my money out and was handing it to Jake when Danny abruptly pushed my hand aside and paid the bill.

"Thanks," I said, "but you didn't have to pay. I had it."

"Look," Danny said roughly. "I may not be like all those other guys at the stable, but I can afford to take you out for coffee. Let's just get that straight right from the beginning. Okay?"

I was stunned, but Danny turned and marched out of Jake's before I could respond. I grabbed the coffees and, pushing and shoving my way through the crowd, ran out after him. I finally caught up with Danny at the corner. I stared at him in amazement; he had an incredibly short fuse.

Normally I'd have been too shy to say anything to Danny about what he'd said, but that day I was already at my wits' end. I was feeling torn up about Mirage, and didn't have total control over my own temper. I guess that's what gave me the courage to set him straight.

"You know sometimes you're a real jerk," I yelled. "What's the big deal? I just wanted to thank you for taking all that time with Mirage."

I was stepping off the curb to walk away when Danny grabbed my shoulder and yanked me back onto the sidewalk. Suddenly a beat-up taxicab, horn honking loudly, screeched by, narrowly missing me. For a minute we stood there in complete silence.

The bag of coffee was visibly shaking in my hands as Danny looked at me and smiled. "I didn't want *you* to wear the coffee this time."

He took my hand again and led me across the street. This time, though, he intertwined his fingers with mine. When we got to the other side, he didn't let go, and I certainly didn't either.

"Look," Danny began as we stopped walking. "I'm sorry. I didn't mean to blow up at you. It's just that I wanted to take *you* out. I wanted to treat you, but you beat me to the punch."

I looked up at him. "I'm sorry, too. I've gotten used to taking care of myself. That's all." As I said this, I let go of his hand and reached up to touch his cheek. I don't know why I did it; it just felt like the natural thing to do. "I've gotten pretty good at it, too. I've had to."

Without saying another word he leaned his head forward and kissed me.

At first I was kind of surprised—stunned, I should say—and didn't know how to react. Fortunately my lips quickly took over. It was our first real kiss—*my* first real kiss—and it was just like in the movies—it went on and on and on. While we were kissing, everything else faded into the background. I completely forgot about Mirage, and that we were standing in the middle of a busy New York City sidewalk. When we finally came up for air, Danny took my hand and we started walking again.

On the corner of 89th Street and Columbus Avenue are a bunch of town houses. Even though they're brand new, they're built to look old. Between the town houses and Parkside Stables is a community garden. For years, the neighbors had maintained and used it as a common produce garden. Recently, however, a block association had turned it into a minipark complete with a beautiful flower garden and wooden benches.

Danny and I headed into the park and sat down on a bench that was tucked beneath a large maple tree. I'd been feeling shy with Danny all along, and as the tension about Mirage faded from my mind, the shyness came on full force. It's weird, but I think I was also feeling embarrassed by our kiss. I couldn't think of a thing to say to Danny. I guess he was feeling a little awkward, too, because we sat in silence, looking into our cups and sipping our coffee.

Suddenly, I remembered how my mother had once told me that one way out of an awkward silence was to ask a person about himself. By now it was clear I wasn't going to spout out anything particularly clever.

"So," I said, "tell me about yourself."

Danny shrugged. "What's to tell?" he asked. "I'm just a regular guy, with a regular life, and a regular family. My mom and dad have been married forever. I've got three older brothers and would probably have at least three younger ones if my mom had her way." Danny looked at me kind of sheepishly. "She stopped at four, but I think she really wanted a little girl and would have put up with as many of us guys as it took to get one."

"So why'd she stop?" I couldn't believe I had asked that amazingly stupid question. Somehow around Danny I seemed to say the dumbest things.

"Babies cost money, you know," Danny said, with a tight look on his face. It was more of a sad face than an angry one. "I guess my folks decided that four hungry mouths were enough to feed."

I nodded and looked away. The garden was spectacular. All the trees were flowering, and it seemed as though the whole world was in bloom. "I guess it must have been hard," I finally said, "but, well, I think you're lucky. All those brothers. I would love to have older brothers."

I thought about how lonely it was sometimes since my dad had left, and how scary it had been when my parents used to fight before the divorce. I sighed. "It would have been so great to have siblings," I said. Then, realizing how pathetic I sounded, I tried to make a joke out of it. "But at least I have Mirage!" I think that was the first time I realized that having a horse wasn't the same thing as having a brother or sister. Mirage was a wonderful friend, but he wasn't a person. I couldn't share my hopes and dreams with him.

"Siblings aren't so great, not when you're the youngest. I had hand-me-down everything. Even my diapers were secondhand. Still," Danny added, "we do have a good time together . . . now that we're older, that is."

He tossed his empty coffee cup into a nearby trash can before continuing. "And I do love working with my dad in the summers. It's better than college. He's taught me so much I'd never have had the chance to learn. All my brothers have worked with him at one time or another."

"What does your mom do?" I asked.

"Do?" he asked, looking at me as if I'd just asked him which bank his mother had robbed lately or something. "What do you mean 'do'? She's a mom. You know, with four boys and my father, she's got a full-time job. My oldest brother moved out a year ago, but the other two are still living at home."

I sighed. "I envy you having a mother and a father. It must be so nice to come home to a . . . a family."

Danny gave me a gentle smile. "Do you want to tell me what happened? With your folks, I mean?"

I finished my coffee and started picking at the Styrofoam rim of the cup. This wasn't exactly something I talked about much. In fact, I'd barely ever discussed it with Susan.

"Well, for one thing, I haven't seen my dad in almost two years," I started, taking a deep breath. It was still hard for me to talk about it. "He had this . . . uh . . . girlfriend and, well, one day he came home and packed his things and left. The next thing I knew, my parents were divorced. End of family, end of story."

"Sounds more like the beginning of the story," Danny said as he put his hand on my arm. "So, what does your dad do?"

"Yeah, well, my dad was a doctor. . . . I mean, he is a doctor. An internist. When my folks were married, we lived in a really nice penthouse overlooking the river. My mom worked for the fun of it. You know, just something to keep her busy. But everything changed when he left."

I leaned back on the bench and looked around the park. This was harder than I thought. "Mom and I had to move into a little apartment, just a couple of blocks from the stable. She has a new job, and now it's our sole means of support. She wouldn't take alimony. She was trying to show my dad that she didn't need him for anything." I took another deep breath. "That's why all those cracks of yours about my being a rich kid really hurt my feelings."

"I didn't know," Danny said gently. "I'm sorry."

"That's okay. I guess you had no way of knowing," I said. Then I went on. "Anyhow, now my dad sends me post-cards from California—that's where he lives—every once in a while. He called me on my last birthday." I made a face. "This year he was only a day late. He sends us the court-ordered child-support payments every month, but it's not very much money."

"It must be really tough on you and your mom," Danny said.

I just shrugged my shoulders and tried to smile. "The past two summers I had a full-time job and didn't have too much fun. Mom wanted me to enjoy the time I have before I go away to school, so she said I didn't have to work this summer. It was my graduation present from her."

"Sounds like your mom is pretty cool," Danny said.

"Yeah, she is," I agreed. "You know, I have to give up Mirage at the end of summer. We can't afford my college tuition and a horse. I'm giving him to Susan. At least then I'll be able to ride him when I come home on vacations."

I paused for a minute, thinking about how nasty I'd been to Susan that morning. "I blamed Susan for hurting Mirage," I whispered. "I was so awful."

"Come on, let's take a walk," Danny said, jumping to his feet. He reached down and pulled me off the bench. "We're getting too gloomy sitting here!"

He took my hand, and we headed out of the little park and over to Columbus Avenue. "So," he said, "where are you going to school in September?"

"State College, the one in Ithaca," I said, shrugging. I wasn't too thrilled about going there, but it was my best choice. "Know it?"

"Know it? You're kidding, right?" Danny asked incredulously. "We're going to be neighbors."

I glanced up at him with a puzzled look on my face.

"I'm a junior at Delany," he said.

I was impressed. Delany was one of the toughest schools to get into in the entire country.

"Full scholarship," he added. "My apartment's less than ten minutes from that bastion of higher education, State. Isn't that great?"

I nodded. "Yeah," I said, trying to sound unexcited. Immediately, I had visions of Danny and me on campus. Studying in the library, cheering at football games, spending romantic evenings in his apartment . . . I was really getting ahead of myself.

"So, what are you going to study?" he asked, interrupting my fantasy.

"Well, I want to major in journalism," I babbled. "I figure I can get a job after college writing for one of the horse publications, like *Equis*. But State doesn't have a journalism program, so I figure I'll go liberal arts for the first two years and then try for a scholarship at a private school that does have a journalism program."

Danny said something else that I missed because all I could think about was that we were going to be living near each other in the fall. I felt more cheerful already.

"I'm sorry. What did you say?" I asked, embarrassed.

"I asked if you meant a private school like Delany?" Danny had a teasing look on his face.

"Who knows?" I said with a sly grin. "So what are you studying?"

"See, I knew you weren't listening when we were up in Mirage's stall. I told you I was a veterinarian in training."

"I'm sorry." I felt as if I kept apologizing to him. "I didn't mean not to listen to you. It's just that I was so upset . . ."

Danny shook his head. "Hey, you don't have to explain anything." He grinned and started with that funny accent again. "Ze brilliant doctor hears all, sees all, and understands all!"

I laughed. "I know you'll be great," I assured him. "If I were any good at science I'd study to be a vet. I can't imagine a more fun career. Getting to be with animals all the time—I'd love that. Especially being able to deliver the babies and make sick ones well . . ." I couldn't help thinking about Mirage and wishing I could fix his leg. Once again, tears started to well up in my eyes.

"I can always help you with your science courses next year, you know," he offered.

My heart beat faster at the suggestion. I think we both knew then that this was the beginning of something that could turn out to be very special. I didn't ever remember feeling that way before.

Glancing at my watch, I realized that over an hour had passed since we left Mirage.

"Come on," Danny said as if he had read my thoughts. I looked up into his eyes and saw the same sparkle I had seen when I first said hello to him that day at Parkside. "We'll stop off at the stable before I walk you home. Maybe we'll see my dad and he can check out Mirage."

We walked a little faster, and it took us less than ten minutes to get back to Mirage's stall. There was no sign of Mr. Booth anywhere inside the stable. After checking Mirage one more time, we headed out of Parkside and down Amsterdam Avenue.

Neither of us said much as Danny walked me home. I had a lot on my mind, and judging from his general silence, Danny did, too. As we neared my building, my thoughts shifted from concern about Mirage to anticipation of Danny kissing me again. Unfortunately, when we got to my stoop, Susan was sitting there waiting for me. Boy, I thought *my* eyes looked puffy from crying.

Danny started to say something to Susan but stopped. Instead, he looked at me and said, "I'll be heading on back to the stable. Don't worry, I'll find my dad and make sure he checks on Mirage before we leave tonight. What time will you be in tomorrow?"

"Bright and early," I said, trying to sound cheerful.

"Me, too," Danny said with a wink.

Then he turned and headed down Amsterdam Avenue toward Parkside.

I looked at Susan and smiled weakly. "Uh . . . want to come on up?" I asked.

"Yeah," Susan said quietly and stood up.

We didn't say anything as we headed inside my apartment. Walking up five flights of stairs is not exactly conducive to conversation. Mom was still at the office, so we headed straight to my room and sat down on my bed.

I looked at Susan, and she began to cry immediately. "I'm so sorry," she whimpered between sobs.

Never one to let a friend cry alone, I started blubbering, too. "No, I'm the one who should be sorry," I confessed. "I don't know what got into me. I know you'd never do anything intentionally to hurt Mirage. I know you love him as much as I do."

"Is . . . is he going to be all right?" Susan asked through her tears.

"I don't know," I said, shaking my head. "I . . . I hope so."

After a few more minutes of whimpering and sniffling, we wandered into the

111

kitchen in search of that tried-and-true age-old therapy for the blues . . . ice cream.

"So," Susan said with her mouth full of chocolate-chocolate chip, "what's he like?"

"Who, Danny?"

"No, Mirage. Of course Danny!"

I had to think about this question for a second. I wasn't sure how I wanted to describe Danny. My answer was different than it would have been a couple of hours ago. Earlier, I might have said he was kind of distant or even cold. But not now, no way.

"Oh, he's kind of macho, but really sweet and nice," I said vaguely.

"Macho? Really sweet? Nice? Come on, Julia, tell me everything," Susan pried.

By the time Mom got home, Susan and I had gone through two pints of ice cream and had rehashed my walk with Danny about fifteen times. Susan had decided that this was the "real thing" and was already picking out china and silverware patterns for our marriage. Of course, that's what friends are for!

Mom came into the kitchen and sat down with us at the table. She looked at the empty ice-cream containers. Then she looked from me to Susan and back at me before speaking.

"From the looks of things," she concluded, moving the empty ice-cream containers in front of her, "this must have been some major discussion. Do you want to fill me in? How's Mirage? Is he going to be all right?"

"What's to say?" I wondered aloud. "I won't know what's wrong with Mirage till sometime tomorrow. Danny looked at him this afternoon, and he's going to get his dad to check out Mirage in the morning if he couldn't get to it before they left this afternoon."

I paused and offered up sort of a silent prayer, the way you wish on a star as a kid. "It could be just a sprain or sore joint."

"A sprain or a sore joint is two pints' worth?" Mom said, as she looked at the empty containers.

"Well, actually, Mirage was about this much," Susan said as she pushed the first container at my mother and pointed to

113

the halfway point on the second one. "The rest of the ice cream was devoted to Danny."

I quickly gave Susan a jab in the ribs to silence her, but the damage had already been done.

Mom picked up the empty containers and reached around to toss them in the trash can behind her. "So, how serious is this?" she asked, trying to conceal a smile.

"Uh . . . he's a friend, that's all!" I claimed, defensively. "Geez, he's just a friend!" Mom asked me about guys all the time. She acted as if every guy I ever mentioned was a potential son-in-law.

I didn't want to get Mom's hopes up or make Danny a subject for discussion until I was a little surer of him. Actually, I was worried that if I talked about him any more I might jinx things. Dumb, huh?

Susan opened her mouth but closed it again when she saw the look in my eyes.

"Susan, dear," Mom said, trying to ease the tension that had suddenly developed around the table. "Why don't you stay for dinner." She looked at the ice-cream containers in the garbage. "Although I doubt if either of you are very hungry right now. We can order something in later on."

"Thanks. Let me call my folks and find out if it's okay." Susan got up and headed for the telephone in my bedroom.

"Why don't you spend the night?" I called to her. "Then we can get an early start for the stable tomorrow. Is it okay, Mom?"

"Excellent idea, dear," Mom said. "Go ahead and call, Susan. Julia, how about setting the table?"

"Sure, Mom," I agreed.

I got some plates from the cabinet and silverware from the drawer and began setting the table. Mom came over to me and pulled out a chair.

"Julia, sit down a minute," she ordered gently. "There's something we have to talk about."

I could tell from her tone that this was going to be a serious conversation. She pulled out another chair, and we both sat down.

"Julia," Mom began, "you know how much I love you, and I know how much you love Mirage, but if his injury is bad it could be very expensive. The veterinarian's bill alone could be thousands of dollars. I just don't have that kind of money."

I'd been afraid of even considering this aspect of Mirage's ailment. I knew we couldn't afford even a very minor vet bill. Something requiring any kind of long-term care wasn't even a possibility.

"What about insurance? Doesn't your medical plan cover this?" I asked, hopefully. I knew that I was being silly.

"Julia, my medical plan barely covers our problems. It only pays eighty percent of what they consider are reasonable expenses of dependents' health care. I don't think they'd consider a horse a dependent, no matter how much we love him."

I sat silently staring at my clasped hands, not knowing what to say or think. Mom had laid down the law. If Mirage was sick, he was basically on his own.

"Look, dear," Mom finally said, "Mirage may be absolutely fine tomorrow, so don't worry about it now. I just wanted to prepare you in case Mirage needed more specialized care. That's all."

Even though we didn't have dinner until almost eight o'clock, Susan and I could barely eat a bite. Takeout tacos, burritos, and refried beans mixed with chocolate-chocolate chip ice cream is a singularly unappetizing combination.

That night, I loaned Susan one of my T-shirts to sleep in. I got under the covers, and Susan settled into the trundle bed. She slept over so much that she even kept a toothbrush at the apartment.

"So," Susan said when she had gotten comfortable, "what's it like having a boyfriend?"

I sighed and rolled over so that I could see her. "He's *not* my boyfriend. We just took a walk, that's all."

"Right," Susan argued. "Well, he might become your boyfriend."

"Oh, I don't know, Susan."

"What's not to know? He's nice, he's smart, and he's gorgeous. And I *know* you like him." Susan paused. "Don't you want to go out with him?"

I propped myself up on one elbow and tried to make out her features in the darkness. All I could really see was her smile. "Susan, I don't know *what* I want. I mean I like him, but"—I tried to make a joke out of my insecurity—"you can't miss what you never had."

Susan gave me this blank stare. "What?"

"Look," I said, "I just don't want to get my hopes up. I mean if I like him and we start going out and then he changes his mind or leaves or something, then I'll get hurt. This way—"

"This way you'll be an old maid!" Susan interrupted.

"Susan!"

"Oh, come on, Julia. Get real! Why would he change his mind about liking you? I've known you practically forever, and *I* still like you."

I got out of bed and walked over to my window. I pulled the slats of the mini-blind open and stared out onto the street. "You're not a guy, Susan."

"Really, Julia? Gee, I never noticed before," Susan said sarcastically.

"What I mean is—"

Susan was very serious now when she

cut me off. "I know what you mean, Julia," she said in an exasperated tone. "What you mean is guys leave. Just like your dad, right?"

"Well, he did leave us. And he used to say he loved me and Mom. Mom would've been much better off if she'd never met him!"

"That's not true," Susan argued. "If she hadn't met your dad, she wouldn't have you."

"Forget it," I said. "I really don't feel like having this conversation right now." I got back into bed. "Susan, it's been a long day. Let's talk about something else. Okay?"

Even though she was my closest friend, I didn't feel like telling Susan about what really had happened between Danny and me. That didn't mean I wasn't thinking about it, though. While I chatted with Susan, I kept remembering what it felt like with Danny that afternoon. I relived our discussions and holding his hand, and most of all our kiss.

Susan seemed to respect my not wanting to talk about Danny. We stayed up talking about Mirage until well after midnight. Finally Mom popped her head in the door of my room.

"Girls—" she began.

"I know, Mom." I interrupted her and then in unison Susan and I chanted, "Bedtime!"

It had the desired effect of making Mom laugh. "Okay," she said. "You know," she continued with mock severity, "I need my beauty rest even if you don't. So please keep the giggles to a minimum."

Susan and I whispered for a while, and then she got out of bed and went over to her knapsack.

"What are you doing?" I asked.

She didn't answer. Instead she took her first-place ribbon out of her knapsack and placed it on my dresser near all Mirage's other ribbons and trophies.

"Susan!" I said, surprised. "That's yours. *You* won it."

"No," she said, as she got back into bed. "It's Mirage's. It should stay with his others."

I didn't quite know what to say, so I

just whispered, "Good night." And, although I fell asleep thinking about my horse, it was Danny who filled my dreams.

CHAPTER

SIX

The next morning Danny called me during breakfast. As soon as Susan figured out whom I was talking to, she started making funny faces. I moved into the bedroom, where I could have some privacy, and shut the door. Danny told me that his dad wasn't going to be able to come by to check on Mirage's leg for a couple of days. I was immediately disappointed, partially because I was worried about Mirage, but also because I was hoping that he'd called to ask me out. We talked for a few minutes, then he said that he had to go to work. I think he sensed my disappointment and before hanging up he said, "Just 'cause my dad can't make it, that doesn't mean that I won't be able to come by." True to his word, Danny stopped in to see me and Mirage that afternoon, and the next, and the next.

I don't know what Danny told his father he was doing, but for three afternoons in a row he came to Parkside. Each evening after Danny had checked out Mirage, we'd taken sandwiches up to the fourth floor of the stable. We sat among the old sleighs and saddles and talked until closing time.

Actually, the fourth floor was a nortorious make-out spot. During the summer months the windows were unboarded, and the light and breeze that they allowed in created the perfect romantic atmosphere. The old equipment provided a place to sit, to rest, to whatever . . .

Danny and I, however, confined our activities to talking and eating. Well, there was some hand holding and watching the sun set over the Hudson River. Since that first kiss after the show,

Danny had only given me a good-bye peck on the cheek. He seemed to know that I needed to take things slowly.

By the third night I was ready to progress in the relationship. While we watched the sun go down, I snuggled up against Danny. He put his arm around my waist and turned me to face him. "You know how much I like you," he said in a husky voice. "Don't you, Julia?"

I nodded, and he leaned across to kiss me. Just as his lips grazed mine, we heard Denise's voice.

"Whoops! Sorry!" she said. She was clutching Bill, Jr., by the arm. "Guess this spot is already taken. And look at by who." She turned to Bill. "Or is it whom?"

He shrugged.

"Come on, Julia," Danny said, dragging me to my feet and out the door.

When we got downstairs, Danny put his arm around me. "Some timing those two have, huh?"

I nodded and blushed, but before I could say anything, Danny leaned over and planted a long, gentle kiss on my lips. "See you tomorrow."

"See you," I said, sorry the kiss had ended so soon.

Danny stepped away, but then he stepped back and kissed me again. This time when we broke apart I was out of breath.

The next morning I got to the stable just as it was opening. I'd been keeping an eye on Mirage's lump and hoping it would go down naturally. Sometimes injuries just healed themselves. But Mirage's lump wasn't going away. Actually, it had grown a bit since the show. I was grooming Mirage when Susan came flying into his stall. "Julia, quick, fix your hair," she blurted out.

"Susan, quick, why?" I teased her.

" 'Cause Danny and his dad just pulled up and when Mr. Booth got out of the truck, I heard Danny say that you were probably upstairs. Then he told him that he'd meet him at Mirage's stall.

"Wait a minute," I said, confused. "Who's meeting whom where?"

Susan grabbed one of Mirage's brushes, and, too impatient to explain again, started to brush my hair.

I wasn't exactly crazy about this. Mirage was my pal and everything, but the idea of using his brush grossed me out a little. Also, my curly hair would become a giant frizz-ball if Susan succeeded in brushing it. I tried to wrestle the brush out of her hand, and Susan fought just as hard to get it through my hair. Suddenly we both froze. We could hear Danny's voice as he came up the ramp.

" 'Bye!" Susan said, dropping the brush and scurrying down the aisle. "Good luck," she whispered, as she ducked into Thunder's stall.

"Honestly!" I muttered. "Oh hi, Danny . . . hi, Mr. Booth." I was trying to sound surprised. I have no idea why. It just seemed like the thing to do.

Danny came over to my side and casually draped his arm over my shoulder. "Julia, you know my dad, don't you?" Danny must have been a little nervous. He knew that I'd known Mr. Booth for years.

I slid out from under Danny's arm but smiled at both him and his father. "Of course I do," I said to Danny.

"Hi, Julia." Mr. Booth smiled at me. "How's Mirage doing today?"

I shrugged. "He doesn't seem to be in any pain," I said. "But the lump's gotten a little bigger," I added with a frown.

"Tell you what, why don't you scoot out of the way and I'll take a look at our patient for you."

"All right, Mr. Booth," I said, stepping out of the stall.

"Danny, hold on to Mirage's halter for me, will you?" Mr. Booth asked.

Danny went into the stall with his dad. He held Mirage still while Mr. Booth patted Mirage's neck. Mirage knew him well from all the times the farrier had shod him. Mirage playfully nuzzled at Mr. Booth's pocket.

"Want your sugar, do you?" Mr. Booth laughed. He always had treats for the horses, giving them one before and after working on them.

"Mirage, you stop that!" I scolded mildly. I hated it when Mirage showed just how few manners he had. But I guess you can't expect a horse to have studied etiquette or attended charm school.

"Don't worry about it, Julia," Mr. Booth said, as he reached into his pocket for a lump of sugar.

After Mirage had wolfed down his goodie, Mr. Booth began examining his leg. He bent down and ran his hand over Mirage's knee. He furrowed his brow and shook his head as he felt the lump. All of a sudden my stomach knotted, and I felt as if I was going to get sick.

Mr. Booth stood up and turned toward Danny. "Let's take him down into the arena and trot him so I can see how he's going," he suggested. "Want to come, Julia?"

I nodded and stepped back into the stall. My throat had gotten all tight. I knew I was probably overreacting, but I still didn't trust myself to speak.

Hooking Mirage's lead rope onto his halter, I led him down the aisle and ramp into the arena. I waited until Mr. Booth and Danny had climbed onto the mounting block, then I walked Mirage around in a circle. Susan had crept halfway down the ramp and was intently watching me put Mirage through his paces.

"Okay, Julia," Mr. Booth called out after I had walked Mirage for a minute or so. "Take him at a trot."

As I started to trot Mirage, I could tell

from the feel of the lead rope and the uneven sound of the hoofbeats that his condition hadn't improved any. He was still lame.

"That's enough, Julia," Mr. Booth said. "We'll meet you upstairs." Danny and his dad hopped off the block and headed up the ramp.

I stopped Mirage and gently stroked his neck as I whispered in his ear. "You're going to be fine, boy. Just fine," I assured him, scratching behind his ear. He butted me with his head, nearly knocking me off balance. I laughed. "Unless you do that again, you big dummy!"

I grabbed his lead rope and led him carefully up the ramp. I could hear Mr. Booth talking to Danny as Mirage and I made our way down the aisle to his stall.

When Mirage and I got back to the stall, Mr. Booth stopped talking and turned to me. "Well, young lady, I guess you have your work cut out for you."

"What do you mean?" I asked. "Is Mirage going to be okay?" I held my breath as I waited for his answer. I could see Susan peering around the doorway of the stall. She held up her hands to show me that her fingers were crossed.

"I'm not a vet, Julia," Mr. Booth began. "But there are a couple of things you should try before calling one. It'll be hard work, but I think it'll pay off."

I nodded. Even though he wasn't a doctor, Mr. Booth knew more about horses than anyone I knew. He suggested making a poultice to draw heat to the leg and then wrapping the foreleg. The bandage would have to be changed four times a day, which was what he meant by "work." As far as I was concerned, if the poultice was going to help Mirage, I'd be happy to change it as often as necessary. Even if that meant staying all night at Parkside and getting up every hour on the hour!

"Come on, Danny," Mr. Booth said, after he'd given me a list of the ingredients for the mixture. "We've got other work to do."

"But . . ." Danny began.

"No 'buts,' son," Mr. Booth said in a tone that left no room for argument or discussion. "We still have to check on the rest of the horses. That reminds me,

Laura left word that Money threw a shoe. Don't worry, you can come back up and help your lovely lady later on."

I went bright red when he said 'lovely lady,' but I liked the sound of it, too. It meant that Danny had mentioned our relationship to his dad.

"See you later, Mr. Booth," I said. "Thanks for coming."

"No problem," he said. "Take care of that horse. I'll be back to check on him in a day or two."

As soon as Danny and his father were gone, I decided to get started mixing what I hoped would be the magical potion that would speed Mirage's recovery.

Susan walked with me to the end of the aisle where the first-aid stall was located. We went inside to get the ingredients I'd need to make the poultice. It took us about a half hour or so to make the foul-smelling paste. When we'd finished, we returned to my stall and wrapped Mirage's leg. Through it all, Susan, who had eavesdropped on my entire conversation with Mr. Booth and Danny, kept teasing me.

"Can I help, lovely lady?" she asked

with a laugh. "Does the lovely lady need anything else? My, what a lovely-looking snack," she said, sniffing the poultice. "Mind if I try a bit?"

I finally had to tell her in no uncertain terms to shut up or else. It's not that I wanted to be mean or I didn't have a sense of humor, it's just that I wanted to savor that moment of recognition, not joke about it.

Susan became serious. "Look, this is the perfect time for you to ask Danny over for dinner and a movie at your place. Didn't you say your mom was going out tomorrow night?"

"Yeah, but I don't know if it's such a good idea," I answered hesitantly.

"Come on, Julia! You know he's really into you. Either that or he's romantically interested in your horse!" She gave me an evil-looking grin.

I started to laugh. "Susan . . ."

"Then again," she continued in a teasing voice as she got right up close to Mirage's face, "Mirage *is* kinda cute! Can he dance?"

"Stop!" I giggled. "I'll do it." I paused and added, "Maybe!"

"You can say it's just your way of saying thank you," Susan suggested. "If you're too chicken to admit that you want him all to yourself . . ."

"Susan, I am *not* chicken!" I insisted. "I'll show you. I'll go ask him. Okay?"

"Okay! Fine! Go ahead, do it! Now!" She pointed down the aisle toward the arena.

"Fine. I will." I handed her Mirage's currycomb. "You finish looking after Mirage. I'll be right back. And while I'm gone, I want you to clean out the stable and curry him till his coat shines. Got that, Cinderella?" I joked.

"Got it!" Susan was grinning as I stomped out of the stall.

I stopped at the top of the ramp to think about what I was going to say. I must have run through about sixty different ways of asking "Do you want to come over for dinner?", before I decided to go with the direct route.

I practiced saying to myself, "Danny, my mom's going out tomorrow night— would you like to come over for dinner?" as I walked down the ramp.

But when I got to the bottom, I was in

for the shock of my life. It was as though someone had slapped me in the face. Danny was standing there with his arm around the shoulders of the most beautiful girl I'd ever seen.

She could have walked right off the cover of a fashion magazine. From her perfectly straight, white teeth to her shiny blond hair, she was absolutely gorgeous.

She was tall, statuesque, and her hair was long, blond, and *straight.* I imagined that it went *whoosh* when she turned her head. Mine just sort of goes *boing.* And, boy, did she have a great figure. I'd die to be built like that.

They were talking quietly, then Danny leaned close to her and said something in her ear. She burst out laughing. Then he grabbed her and gave her this great big hug. I was getting angrier and angrier by the minute. And that's when he did it. He kissed her on the lips.

Danny hadn't spotted me, even though I was only about twenty feet away. I quickly turned around and ran back up the ramp. Susan didn't look up from where she was kneeling as I dashed into the stall.

"So," she asked, "how'd it go? Do you have a date with . . ."

"NO!" I shouted. "And I don't want one. I hate him! That . . . that . . ."

"HUH?" Susan dropped the grooming tool and whirled around so fast, she fell backward onto the hay that we used for Mirage's bedding. "Excuse me, are we talking about the same guy? What happened, Julia? What's wrong? Didn't you ask him over?"

"No, as a matter of fact I didn't!" I said bitterly. My face was bright red—not the nice kind of red that comes from blushing but the horrible blotchy kind that comes from anger and embarrassment.

"He was busy—very busy!"

"Busy?" Susan looked confused. "What are you talking about? Come on, Julia, speak to me! What on earth is going on?"

"Look," I said. "He was with this girl, this absolutely great-looking girl—"

"So?" Susan interrupted.

"So?" I asked. I couldn't believe she

didn't know what I meant. Nobody could be that dense.

"So, maybe she's a boarder or one of the new instructors."

"No way! I know all of them, and she wasn't. Besides, why would he kiss and hug a boarder or a new instructor? Huh? Can you answer me?"

"Well," Susan said sensibly, "you're a boarder and . . ."

"You're not helping, Susan!" I said through clenched teeth. I was really getting steamed.

"I'm out of here," Susan said. "I'm going to see what's happening for myself."

"Susan, wait!" I yelled after her. Before I could stop her, she ran out of the stall and down the aisle toward the ramp.

Actually, I didn't want to stop her from leaving. I wanted to be alone. I felt like a fool, and I was so angry. I was only partially mad at Danny. Mostly, I was angry at myself for trusting him—and for believing that just because we'd hung out together, and held hands, and kissed once or twice that there was something really going on between us. After all, Danny was in college; he probably kissed girls all the time.

Although I know better now, at that moment all I could see was what a jack-ass I'd been for opening myself up to a guy. I knew better than that. Hadn't I learned anything from my parents?

What I didn't know was what was going on in the arena while I was upstairs feeling sorry for myself. Susan had stormed down into the ring and bounded over to Danny and the girl. Danny described the scene to me later.

"Would you excuse us for a minute?" Susan had said to Danny's unknown female friend.

"Susan!" Danny answered with a trace of annoyance in his voice.

"Please! I need to talk to Danny. Now!" Susan was ignoring Danny and talking directly to the girl.

"Uh, sure," the girl said, puzzled. She turned back to Danny. "Listen, I have to get going anyway. My car's double-parked right in front of the door. But promise you won't forget about next weekend, Danny."

"Sure, Alissa. I'll call you at home,"

Danny called out to her as she hurried away. Then he turned his attention back to Susan.

"Susan, now what's all this—" Danny began.

"Exactly," Susan cut him off. She stood facing him with her hands on her hips.

"What?" Danny asked again.

"You know!"

"Susan! I have no idea what you're so worked up about." Poor Danny. He wasn't very experienced with Susan's shorthand way of speaking.

"I thought you liked Julia," Susan said.

"I do," Danny answered indignantly.

"Then who was *she*?" Susan demanded.

"'She'?" Danny started looking left and right. Then he stopped and started to laugh. "'She'?"

"I'm glad you find this all so funny," Susan snapped. "I fail to see the humor in any of it."

Now here's where things went wrong. If Susan had stuck around to hear Danny's explanation and then had told me what he'd said, everything would

139

have been cleared up. But Susan, loyal friend that she is, was so upset for me that she burst into tears and left Danny standing there completely baffled.

I was still in Mirage's stall brushing his coat when Danny came thundering up the ramp.

"We need to talk!" he ordered, as he reached Mirage's stall.

"About what?" I asked, trying to sound casual.

"Look. She's just—" he began.

"You don't owe me an explanation," I interrupted. I was very aware of just how nasty I was being.

Suddenly there was complete quiet. "No," Danny said after a moment's pause. "You're right, I don't!" And with that, he walked away from the stall.

As soon as he was out of sight, I burst into tears. I had hoped I'd been wrong about Danny, but at that moment I was convinced that I was right about what I'd told Susan. There was absolutely no point in trusting men!

CHAPTER
SEVEN

I didn't see Susan for the rest of that day, but the following day when we hooked up at the stable, we made a deal not to talk about Danny.

"I just don't want to dwell on what a jerk I was," I told her. "Okay, Susan?"

"But you weren't a jerk, Julia," she insisted. "He was."

"No, it was me," I said, absently running a hand over Mirage's mane. "I was the one who got my hopes up. Promise me, though, you won't bring it up."

"Fine," she agreed, with a sigh. "I promise."

It was bizarre. Susan and I had never had a shortage of things to talk about before, but now that there was this one forbidden subject, neither of us had anything to say. We ended up just focusing on Mirage.

The next few days were unbelievably boring. One afternoon I saw Mr. Booth's truck out in front of the stable, but I stayed upstairs until it pulled away. Danny wasn't exactly making a big effort to find me, either.

Susan and I changed Mirage's poultice four times a day as Mr. Booth had instructed. It was hard to tell if the paste was helping him at all. Of course, I couldn't ride Mirage. Instead of exercise, he received hours of daily rubdowns and a whole lot of loving attention.

Every horse owner has to learn how to do rudimentary vet stuff for her horse. No matter how much money you have, it just doesn't make sense to call in a vet for a simple problem that you can treat yourself. It's like when you have a little cold or a slightly twisted ankle, you don't go running off to a doctor. Calling a vet whenever the slightest thing goes wrong would be like going to the dermatologist for every single pimple.

By the end of the week Mirage seemed to be improving. The swelling on his leg had gone down a little. Although I still hadn't put any weight on his back for a few days, I thought it would be okay to saddle him up and put him on the lunge line.

A lunge line is about twenty feet long. You snap it onto the bridle or halter and, standing in the center of the ring, walk or trot the horse in a circle around you. To keep the horse moving, some people use a long whip which they crack behind the horse's haunches. Mirage was voice trained, which means that all I had to do was to tell him to walk, trot, canter, or *whoa*.

After putting on his halter and attaching the lead rope, I eased Mirage down the ramp and into the arena. I had to wait until a beginners' lesson was finished before I could let out the lunge line to begin working him.

The biggest danger for a horse who's

been laid up is the first workout. After being penned up for a while, sometimes a horse will go a little nuts and hurt himself. It's like with a little kid. You keep them in bed when they're sick, and then the first day they're allowed out of bed, they overdo it and get sick again.

Mirage hadn't been out of his stall for almost a week. He was a bundle of energy, and I didn't want him straining too hard during his first workout.

Normally, I just hooked the clip of the lunge line onto the halter, but that day I took the time to run the chain part of the line through the halter itself so that if he got out of control I could give it a sharp tug. The chain would press down on his nose; it was supposed to make him calm down and pay attention. I was hoping it wouldn't be necessary, but I knew it was kinder to hurt him a little in order to prevent him from hurting himself a lot. Still, I hated to do it.

I walked Mirage in both directions for a while to loosen up his stiff muscles. Then we got down to some serious work. I'd trotted Mirage for about fifteen minutes and was cooling him down when Danny walked into the arena.

"He looks pretty good," he said, strolling over to Mirage. Danny pulled a sugar cube out of his pocket and let Mirage take it out of his palm. Then he walked around to Mirage's haunch and ran his hand over his croup, the area on a horse's rear just above the tail. "How is he at the trot?"

"Fine," I said. On the outside I was playing it cool, but on the inside I was grinning. I'd missed Danny. I wasn't sure whether my excitement was because Danny was there or because of the state of Mirage's health. It was probably a lot of both.

"I'm going to put him away now," I said, walking over to Mirage and unhooking the lunge line from the halter.

"Can I help?" Danny offered.

"Sure." I shrugged. "If you don't have anything else to do."

Together we took Mirage upstairs to his stall.

"Look," Danny said when we got inside. "We need to talk. That was my cousin the other day."

"It's really none of my business," I started to say.

"Hey, wait a minute. I thought we were friends," he said. "You should have asked me about it before getting all bent out of shape."

"I just thought . . ."

"You just thought I was a jerk leading you on?"

I didn't say anything.

"Listen, I'm not a jerk," he insisted. "I could understand Susan not trusting me, but you? I mean I know we only met each other a few weeks ago, but I thought you knew me better than that." Danny looked hurt and angry. Now I felt really dumb.

"I'm sorry," I said. "You're right. I jumped to the wrong conclusion."

We just looked at each other for a minute. "Okay," he said. "Apology accepted." He gave me a mock scowl. "But don't ever let it happen again."

I held up my hand in the girl scout salute. "I promise."

Danny unbuckled Mirage's girth and eased off his saddle and saddle pad as I attached the chain across the opening of the stall. I turned around to take off Mirage's bridle at the same time that Danny reached for it.

It was as though everything happened in slow motion. His hand closed over mine. I could feel the smooth leather of the halter under my fingers and his rough, callused fingers on top of my hand. I couldn't hear anything except for my heart pounding in my ears, and I couldn't think about anything except wanting to kiss Danny.

Suddenly, he took my hand off the bridle and pulled me toward him. Somehow, I'd never realized how tall he was; my head barely came up to his shoulder.

He cupped my chin and turned my face to his. At that moment, his eyes were the deepest blue that I'd ever seen. I rose up on my tiptoes and Danny leaned down. As our lips met, his hand caressed my cheek. When we drew apart, he gently ran his fingers over my lips. Then he kissed me softly once again.

He pulled away and smiled at me. "I'm glad Mirage is okay," he said softly. "See you tomorrow." He ducked under the chain and walked down the aisle.

We'd kissed before, and they were great kisses, too, but there was something different about this kiss—something bigger and more intense. Maybe our fight made us realize how much we really meant to each other. By the time I got my brain reactivated and my feet moving, he was gone.

"Julia! Julia! Hey, Julia!" Susan had obviously been trying to get my attention for some time. "*Yoo-hoo!* Anybody home?"

"Susan. Sorry. OHMYGOSH! Guess what. Come here! Quick!" I dragged Susan out of the aisle and into the stall with Mirage. "You'll never in a million years guess. It was wonderful. I thought I would die. Danny . . ."

"You guys made up. Right?"

"How'd you guess?" I wondered if I had a sign on my back or something.

"Well, Danny just passed me on the ramp. He didn't even see me!" Susan laughed. "Besides, he had lipstick on his mouth and I don't really think it's his color!"

She looked at me more closely now.

"It does, however, seem to be yours. And what a surprise, yours is all smeared!"

I wiped my mouth with the bottom of my T-shirt. "Better?"

"Yup. So . . . ?" I still hadn't told Susan about the other time I'd kissed Danny. "Was it incredibly romantic? Were his eyes open? Were yours? Did he use his tongue? Did you? Were there bells? Rockets? Gunfire? I'll bet he's an absolutely fantastic kisser. Am I right? Huh? Oh come on, Julia, talk!"

"Susan! You know, you watch much too much TV. I think I'll have to speak to your parents about it."

Susan didn't say anything, but I knew she was dying of curiosity.

"It was amazing," I dreamily conceded. "He's just . . . I don't know . . . It was so-o-o . . ."

"Come on, Julia. You can do better than that. I want details!"

I was about to tell her everything when we heard Denise, Penny, and Laura laughing as they came up the ramp. The rest of our little discussion was going to have to be postponed until the other girls left.

"So, uh, Penny, when's the party?" Denise's voice carried from her horse's stall on the other side of the floor.

Every summer for the last four years, Penny's parents allowed her to throw a "First Weekend in August Blowout." It was the biggest social event of the summer, and we all eagerly looked forward to it.

Susan and I had gone together to the last three parties. Each summer the event seemed to get increasingly fancier. This year Penny had said that it was going to be a theme party—a costume ball.

I wasn't too excited by the concept. I knew that Laura, Penny, and Denise had already bought very expensive, fancy costumes. That was clearly out of the question for Susan and me. I mean, one of their outfits could pay for an entire semester of college.

"A costume party. How sweet," Mom had said when I told her about the bash. She'd used that really annoying "mother tone."

"Mom, it's not some dumb party. It's a *ball*," I'd protested, "a real costume ball. And I have to have a real costume."

"Look," Mom had said, rubbing her hands over her eyes. "we'll make something—as we did a couple of Halloweens ago."

"MOM!" I had jumped up from the kitchen table. "The last time I celebrated Halloween was when I was twelve. That's not a couple of years ago; it's over five years ago. I was just a little kid then. Besides, everyone is going to be renting these great costumes. I just *can't* go in some dumb old sheet and call myself a ghost! It won't work."

"I don't know what you want me to do," Mom had said angrily. "You know we don't have the money for a fancy costume. If you can't think of something we can afford, then don't go! It's that simple! The choice is yours, Julia."

I'd run crying from the kitchen and hadn't raised the subject since. Mom had a point about the money and all that, but it wasn't my fault we were broke. I felt as if, once again, I was the one being made to suffer because of Mom's refusal to accept alimony.

I had to change schools. I had to move. And I was going to have to give up

Mirage. I always seemed to be suffering because of what someone else did.

"I have the greatest outfit!" Susan and I heard someone saying. It was Penny, of course. Susan and I looked at each other and shrugged. We had decided that we were either going to go as equestrians in our show outfits or dressed regularly, as people who didn't know it was a costume party. Not ideal, but at least it was something we could afford.

This was the first year that Susan and I weren't going as a "couple." Before our fight, Danny had already agreed to be my date. Susan was going to ask some guy in her class at school.

"Let's see what's going on," I suggested to Susan.

"So, what are you going to do about your little problem?" we heard Laura ask as we walked down the aisle.

"I'm not sure," Penny answered. "I don't know what to say to her."

"Well, why don't you just . . ." Laura stopped as she saw Susan and me approach.

"Oh. Hi, Julia. Susan." Denise waved as she filled a water bucket from the spigot outside of her horse's stall. "How's Mirage?"

"Better," I said cheerfully. "Thanks. What's going on, guys?"

"Not much," Laura said, poking her head out of the stall. "We're going for a ride. Wanna come?"

"Sure! I'll go get Thunder tacked up." Susan stopped and looked at me. "Are you coming?"

"I can't," I said. "Not yet. Maybe tomorrow. I don't want to overtax Mirage too soon." I glanced over at Susan, who still seemed unsure. "Go ahead. I'll groom Mirage and hang around till you guys get back. Then we can go get something to eat."

I took Susan's arm and walked her over to Thunder's stall. "Come on. I'll help you get him ready."

When we got into the stall we looked at each other. *"Problem?"* we mouthed silently to each other.

"I didn't know Penny had any problems," I whispered to Susan.

"If she does, she's sure to make them someone else's," Susan joked. It's not that we didn't like Penny. We did. She was okay. It's just that we knew her weaknesses.

Susan and the others mounted up and rode out, leaving me to groom Mirage. When I'd finished, I went down to the mounting block to watch the lessons in the arena.

Sometimes you can pick up a free hint or two if there is a really good rider taking a lesson. Unfortunately, all that was going on now were two beginner lessons —what we call "Up! Downs!" because the instructor spends most of the time shouting "UP! DOWN! UP! DOWN!" to the students as they learn how to post to the trot.

I ended up just letting my mind wander, and although I started with the best of intentions, all I thought about was Danny.

CHAPTER

EIGHT

The weather in New York is, to say the least, very unpredictable. One day it might be eighty degrees with almost no humidity, a sort of "it's-great-to-be-alive" day, and the next it can be so hot you don't want to go outside. The cops call it "killing weather," because when the humidity begins to equal the temperature, people start to go crazy.

When I woke up that morning, it was clearly one of *those* days. I took a cold shower and by the time I'd dried off, the back of my neck was already sticky with

155

sweat. It was too hot for boots and britches, so I slipped into a faded pair of jean shorts and Keds, no socks. I pulled a white tank top from my drawer and slipped it on. It was last summer's favorite shirt, but I found, to my surprise, that I'd, uh, *grown* significantly since then. There was no way I could leave the house in the skimpy shirt.

Actually, out of all of the changes that were happening in my life that summer, it was the only one that didn't have me bummed out. I had been waiting for it to happen since my classmate, Dana Davis, had gotten *her* first bra in fourth grade. As far as I was concerned, it was about time!

I rummaged around the pile of clothes that always seemed to be on the floor of my closet until I came up with a yellow V-necked T-shirt. Grabbing a pair of scissors from my vanity top, I quickly turned it into a sleeveless crop top.

Mom was already in the kitchen making coffee when I got there. I grabbed a mug that had "I'd Rather Be Riding" printed on it and reached for the coffeepot.

"Wait 'til the coffee is finished brewing, please," Mom said.

I leaned against the edge of the sink and set down my mug.

Mom gave me a quick once-over. "Isn't that a new T-shirt?"

"Not new, modified," I corrected. "I didn't have anything cool enough to wear, so I cut up an old T-shirt." I looked away. "I've, uh, kind of outgrown a lot of my tops."

"I've noticed," Mom said. "Maybe we'll go shopping this week and see if we can find some new bras and a top or two for you. Sound good?"

For some reason I found the subject a little embarrassing. Her observation made me blush, but I was thankful for the offer.

Mom smiled and gave me hug. "Are you having a good summer?" I could tell from the look in her eyes that it wasn't a casual question.

I nodded. "Pretty good, Mom. Thanks again. I mean, you know, the summer off and all that."

"I just wish I could give you—"

"Me too, Mom, but it doesn't matter," I cut her off. "Really."

I was perfectly comfortable talking about Mom's social life or, rather, the lack of it, but it always made me nervous when the subject changed to *my* social life or personal stuff.

I guess that right after the divorce I knew that Mom had enough to deal with, so I stopped burdening her with my problems. I figured I could handle them myself.

Anyhow, things were getting too heavy for so early in the morning, so I gave my mom a hug and, figuring that I'd pick up a coffee at Jake's, headed out the door. I walked down the stairs to our building and slowly made my way toward Parkside. It was too hot and gross to do anything quickly.

When I got to the stable, I saw Susan in the arena working Thunder. I waved to her and ran upstairs to check on Mirage. He'd been a little off the day before and I was worried about him.

He was eating when I got to his stall. I reached into his feed basket for a handful of oats and joined him in a little breakfast. I know this sounds disgusting, but it's the same kind of oats that are in granola.

It was not until after Mirage had finished eating his oats that I noticed the envelope with my name on it pinned to the wall. I had a pretty good idea what was in it. I was thrilled, nonetheless, when I ripped it open and saw my invitation.

Just as Penny's parties had gotten increasingly fancy, so had her invitations. This one was embossed in frilly script:

HOORAY!
It's Time Again. . . .
Penny's Fourth Annual
1st Weekend in August Blowout
575 Park Avenue, Penthouse
8 P.M. Until Exhaustion
Come in Costume
RSVP

At the bottom of the invitation, Penny had written: "B.Y.O.B.," which meant Bring Your Own Boy.

As I said, this was the first year I had a boy to bring. Since our rocky start I'd seen a lot of Danny, but we mostly had hung around the barn or gone out to movies. I was kind of nervous about the party. I wasn't exactly sure how to act with a date at a big, fancy get-together. Still, I was really excited to be going with Danny. I also wanted to show off what a handsome and nice boyfriend I had.

I flew downstairs to find Susan. Thunder's owner was riding him, and Susan was sitting on the mounting block watching.

"Which guy are you taking? And what are we going to wear?" I blurted out. "Equestrian or ignoramus? It's your choice." I was sounding like Susan.

She looked at me and pursed her lips. "I'm not going," Susan said, staring straight ahead.

"Oh, come on! It doesn't matter if we don't have fancy costumes." Now that I had Danny, it really *didn't* seem to matter to me. "We'll have fun," I continued. "Besides, we'll be able to make fun of everyone else's costumes."

Susan looked at me as if she wanted to tell me something but didn't know how.

"That's not the point," she said. She looked away, as if she were embarrassed.

"Did your date cancel? You can ask someone else! There must be dozens of guys who'd kill to go out with you."

"That has nothing to do with it," she said.

"Then what?" I had no idea what she was, or rather what she wasn't, talking about.

"Look, it's not the costumes," Susan finally said. "I had a fight with Penny."

I shrugged and looked around the arena. "So, you'll make up. You always do." Penny could be really mean, but usually she apologized afterward.

"Yeah, but *you* won't," Susan said under her breath.

I grabbed her shoulders and turned her to face me. "In English, Susan. Speak slowly and tell me what you're talking about, because right now I'm clueless."

"Okay," Susan said, taking a deep breath. "You know the B.Y.O.B. part of the invitation?" she asked.

I nodded.

"Well, you can't," she said, looking down at her feet.

"What?" I guess I wasn't being particularly quick on the uptake, because I still didn't see where she was heading.

"They asked me . . . no, Penny told me to tell you that you can't bring Danny to the ball."

"Excuse me?" I asked. I couldn't believe what I was hearing.

"He's not . . ." Susan groped for the exact word that Penny and the others had used, ". . . suitable. That was it. They said he wasn't suitable."

I felt myself go really red. Then I became hot, then cold, and then started to sweat. For maybe the first time in my life I was actually speechless.

"I told them that stank," Susan began. "But . . ."

Letting go of Susan's shoulders, I turned away and stared at the invitation in my hand. I burst into tears and tore it into as many pieces as I could before throwing the shredded paper onto the mounting block and sprinting out of the arena.

Until that moment, I really hadn't realized how fully my life had changed since before the divorce. I mean, I knew

162

my dad was gone for good. I knew we had less money. I knew I was different, but I didn't realize how totally alienated from my past life and my past friends I'd become. And now, because I had chosen to be with Danny, I had cut the cord completely. Or maybe it was Penny and the rest who had set *me* adrift . . . cut my cord.

Even in my tearful state, I realized that I wasn't as upset about not going to that stupid party as I was at those snobs thinking that it was okay to exclude Danny because they thought he was low class. Because of the way I felt about Danny, they were excluding *me* as well.

Two years before, when my dad left, my status had changed, but it was at that moment when I became aware that my allegiances had shifted as well. Actually, it wasn't that I had decided to like or dislike people because of money. I found that I was choosing my friends because of *who* they were, not *how much* they had.

"Julia, wait!" Susan yelled to me as I fled.

I tore blindly out of the stables and

onto the sidewalk. I was so angry and felt so betrayed by those prima donnas. Mr. Booth's truck pulled up, but I ignored Danny as he called out my name. I couldn't stop to talk to him now. The way I felt, I had to get as far away from Parkside as possible.

The stable had always been a safe haven to me. After what had just happened, though, it didn't feel safe anymore. It felt ugly and small-minded. It wasn't Parkside itself, but those snobs upstairs, that made me feel that way.

I wanted to collect myself before I told Danny that we weren't going to go to the party. He didn't need to know that he wasn't welcome at the ball; I wanted to protect him. I knew that as far as I was concerned if they didn't want Danny, they didn't want me.

It wasn't until later, however, that Susan told me what happened after I left Parkside. Danny had been really worried when he saw me run out of the stable. He'd gone into the arena to see if he could find Susan, who he figured would know what was wrong with me. He assumed something had happened to Mirage.

"What's going on?" he had asked when he first saw Susan. "Is it Mirage? Is he lame again?"

Susan had looked up at him from her spot on the mounting block and silently shaken her head.

"Is someone sick?" Danny asked frantically. "Susan! What's going on?"

"Look for yourself," she had said, holding out her copy of the invitation. "Look at the B.Y.O.B. part. You know what it stands for?"

Danny had nodded.

"Well, you're the last *B*, except you can't be the *B* because of those stuck-up . . ."

"I'm a beer?" Danny had interrupted, confused. "That's what *B* stands for, right?"

"Not quite," Susan had said patiently. "You're a boy."

"Nice of you to notice," Danny responded dryly.

"Well, those 'friends' of Julia's don't want you to be her *B*."

Suddenly, it clicked for Danny . . .

almost. He started to back away from Susan. "So, they don't want me at the party? A farrier isn't good enough for those pretentious little brats?"

Susan had nodded. "Yeah, but . . ."

"You told Julia." It had been a statement, not a question. "So that's why she ran out of the barn." So far he had been dead-on.

"That's why she didn't stop when I called her name." Unfortunately, here's where Danny's logic made a slight detour. "She doesn't want to have anything to do with me anymore. . . ."

Susan had started to protest, but Danny had already turned away. For the second time in one morning, Susan had been left alone on the mounting block.

I'd run out of the stable with one thought—I needed to be alone. Now, solitude is hard to come by in New York. In fact, the only place I knew of to be alone was my rooftop. So that was where I had headed.

By the time I had climbed the six flights to the roof, I was completely winded. I sank down against the chimney, not realizing at first that I was on the forbidden side of the chimney. I was staring directly into our old apartment.

By now I was reveling in self-pity. I was also really mad at Penny. Oddly enough, even more than that, I was angry at my father.

I'd convinced myself that this incident, and all my other problems, were entirely his fault. And yet, I also knew that he wasn't responsible for Penny's being a jerk any more than he was to blame for Mirage's getting sick. However, I felt that I had to suffer again and again for his selfish actions. That thought only produced a new batch of tears.

I eventually calmed down enough to realize that not only wasn't it my father's fault, but I also didn't want it to be anymore. Making him responsible gave him too much power over my life. I didn't need someone to blame.

Then a weird thing happened. As I got madder and madder at Penny, I got less and less upset about my life in general. Suddenly, the dumb party didn't matter to me, and neither did those dumb girls. I couldn't wait to go back to Parkside and tell Penny what she and her crowd could do with their pretentious ball.

As I left the roof, I felt free of all the things that had been making me feel bad for so long. Free of being upset because I didn't have money. Free of worrying that Danny was going to be like my dad. Free of being dependent on Penny, Denise, and Laura to tell me if I was "cool" or not. Somehow none of that snobby nonsense meant anything to me anymore.

When I got back to Parkside, Danny was outside shoeing one of the stable horses. I knew how puffy my eyes were, but I figured it didn't really matter because he must be used to it by now. After all, that's how he'd seen me most of the time since we met. It had been a difficult summer.

"Hi," I said with a big smile.

Danny barely looked up from the hoof he was working on.

"What are you doing?" It was one of the all-time dumbest questions. I mean, what else would he be doing with a horse's hoof in his lap? But it didn't deserve the answer I got in reply.

"I'm working, Julia." His voice was

dripping with sarcasm. "You know, work. It's that thing that poor people do so that they can eat, and have a place to sleep, and clothes to wear."

I was stunned. "What's going on with you?" I asked. "All I said was 'Hi.' You don't have to be so nasty and bite my head off."

"Look," he said, dropping the horse's hoof. He stood up and glared at me. "I don't owe you an explanation. I don't owe you anything beyond a good job of shoeing. That's all I'm paid for. Got it?"

I could feel the tears well up in my eyes for what seemed like the millionth time that day.

"Oh, and by the way," he continued, "I hope you haven't gotten the wrong idea about us. I never meant to treat you with anything other than professional courtesy. I *do* know the difference in our stations, ma'am!"

"But . . . I thought . . . I mean . . ."

Danny gave me a pitying look. Then he bent down, picked up the horse's hoof again, and went back to work. Forgetting everything I thought I'd learned, I fled to

Mirage's stall in tears. Susan found me sobbing into Mirage's neck.

"Julia, don't cry," she said as she laid a comforting arm around my shoulders.

I've never understood why people always say that. No one ever listens and stops crying. I certainly didn't.

"Seriously, I can't believe you're still crying about the party. They're just a bunch of . . ."

"It's not the party," I managed to gasp out between tears. "It's Danny!"

"I'm sure he'll get over it," she said doubtfully. "I mean, he was pretty irate this morning when I told him—"

"You told him?" I interrupted her. "Susan, think clearly. What did you say to him? Tell me your exact words, please."

"Well, he came over to me to find out what was wrong with you. Anyway, when I told him what Penny had said, he got so mad that he didn't even stick around long enough to find out that you had gotten mad, too."

There was a long pause while I figured things out. "Julia!" Susan exclaimed.

"Why are you smiling? What's going on?"

I gave Susan a hug and told her I'd be right back. It was only a hunch, but I was pretty sure I knew what had happened with Danny. This time he was the one jumping to conclusions. He was the one not giving *me* enough credit. I have to admit, as upset as I was at his behavior, it was nice not being the one acting like a jerk for once.

I ran down the ramp, through the arena, and out to where the truck was parked. Danny was busy taking the shoes off another one of the stable horses.

"Hi." It was my standard greeting—unoriginal but direct.

Danny looked up from what he was doing. "Well, that's a quick recovery. Party plans all set? Found yourself another guy already?"

"You know, you're really sweet," I said, grinning at him.

Now it was his turn to look confused. "Huh?"

"I know what you're doing, and I just want you to know that I'm not going."

"What's the matter, can't get a date?" he asked, sarcastically.

I put my arms around his neck. "Thanks for trying to let me off the hook, but I don't *want* to be let off the hook. And I'm not letting you off the hook, either. We still have a date for the night of the party, and I'm holding you to it."

I was sounding more confident than I felt. I wasn't sure if he'd been trying to let me off the hook or if he was actually mad, but I figured I'd assume the best about someone for a change! It was worth a shot.

Danny looked at me, I mean really looked at me, for the first time that day. I held my breath as I waited to hear what he had to say.

"You mean that? You're sure? I thought this party meant a lot to you." He put his hands on my hips.

"It did." I moved closer to him so that our bodies were touching. "But you mean a lot more."

Danny stared down into my eyes. "Let me guess. I should have had more faith in our relationship and asked you before reacting. Right?"

"Right. If we're going to be together . . ." I began, but his lips smothered the rest of my words.

"Julia," he said as he pulled away. "I want us to be together. But you're not the only one who sometimes gets insecure."

"Okay. So we understand each other?" I could hear the tremor in my voice.

"For now," he said with a smile. "When stuff happens we both need to talk to each other, not run."

I nodded.

"You sure about this?" he asked.

Just then Penny, Laura, and Denise came around the corner on their horses. "Hi, Julia!" they shouted in unison.

I grinned at Danny and planted a big kiss right on his mouth. "Very sure!" I said under my breath. He smiled and kissed me back.

I would have given anything to see the looks on those snobs' faces, but at that moment I was too busy being in Danny's arms to bother looking their way.

CHAPTER

NINE

After the scene with Danny outside the stable, I thought that everything was going to be okay. I knew that Penny and the other girls were going to be in shock that I'd chosen Danny's friendship over theirs, but I figured it would do them some good to be taken down a peg or two. Besides, they were too self-centered to think about it for very long. I had no idea how annoyed they were until weird stuff started happening.

First I couldn't find my water pail, then my grooming tools disappeared.

And, of course, they acted as if I weren't alive. They'd walk right by me and never say a word—not even hello.

"Do you want me to say something to them?" Danny asked one day after we found my grooming tools buried in a pile of hay.

"Why bother?" I asked.

"Julia," Danny said, taking my hand, "that's not the point, and you know it."

I grew serious for a minute. "Look, Danny," I said, "they're going to get bored with this soon enough. We can't prove they're the ones who are doing it."

Danny snorted. "Right! The horses are doing it as a protest about the quality of the hay," he said sarcastically.

I laughed. "You know what I mean. Just let it go." I was so happy with my relationship with Danny that I just didn't have time to feel bad. And those girls definitely weren't worth feeling bad about.

In fact, I felt worse for Susan than I did for myself. After all, I had Danny, and although Susan had me, it was only for another few weeks. At the end of the summer when I went away to college, she'd be left here at Parkside, home of the rich and snobbish.

Even though I was high over Danny, I was also worried about Mirage. He'd be okay for a day or two, and then he'd start to limp again. The lump would go down a bit, and then it would suddenly flare up and be as large as ever. I'd tried all the home remedies I knew. Now it was time to call in the vet.

I had saved up some money for school clothes, but it soon became clear that the only recourse I had left was to spend it on a house call—I mean, a stable call—by Dr. Novegrad.

Dr. Novegrad had been Parkside's on-call veterinarian for more than twenty years. During the summer session of riding camp he gave lectures once a week. He taught the students the proper care and feeding of a horse and simple first aid.

He was known for his great stall-side manner—with both the horses and the owners. He always said that, even though the animals got the medication, the owners usually looked as if they needed it more.

Dr. Novegrad did the same things that Danny and I had done for Mirage. He trotted Mirage to check for the lameness and suggested wrapping the leg and all that stuff. Then he ran some lab tests and took X rays.

We had to wait two days for all the results to come back. No question about it, they were the longest two days of my life. Danny tried to distract me by keeping me guessing about the special date that he'd planned for us that Friday night. He wouldn't tell me what we were going to do or where we were going, but he and Susan kept whispering and giggling about the plans behind my back.

One afternoon Penny and Laura were intentionally talking loudly about the party, just so that I could hear them. Danny and I were in Mirage's stall, and Danny, who was getting angrier and angrier about their behavior, yelled, "Julia, I have something really terrific in mind for our date the night of Penny's extravaganza."

"Danny," I began, "just being together is terrific. I don't need—"

"Hey," he interrupted, "who's in charge of that night? You or me?"

"You are," I answered.

"That's right. And don't you forget it!" He leaned down and kissed me. "Besides, we have something important to celebrate."

"What?"

Danny clutched his heart. "I'm hurt," he said in a mock injured tone.

"Seriously, what?" I asked.

"I can't believe you don't know."

"Danny!"

He grabbed me and we started waltzing around the stall to imaginary music. "Us! Isn't that worth celebrating?"

"Well . . ."

"Enough talk," he said jokingly, then kissed me again.

I didn't get a chance to argue with him, because my mouth was otherwise occupied.

As much as I appreciated and enjoyed Danny's diversions, I still wanted to spend as much time as possible with Mirage.

Mirage didn't limp as long as I didn't put any weight on his back, so I would

179

put his halter on and lead him to the park. We'd walk on the bridle path for a while and then, defying all the rules of the City Parks Commission, I would lead him into this beautiful green meadow just north of Parkside.

A little stream ran through the meadow, and wildflowers blossomed along its banks. It was incredibly peaceful and relaxing. It's strange, but I'm sure Mirage felt better when we were there.

On the day that the results of Mirage's test were due, I took him out for a long afternoon walk.

Susan and Danny had wanted to come with me, but I needed some "quality time" with my oldest friend. I loved Susan like a sister, and I thought I was falling in love with Danny, but it was all a little scary. I needed to get grounded in the one reality I had come to trust over the years: the reality of Mirage as the only one who was always there for me.

We got to the little meadow and sat there for about two hours. Actually, *I* sat there while Mirage grazed.

Watching a horse just being a horse— not a pet or a show pony—is a magical experience. Mirage was truly beautiful, a wonder of nature. He grazed, drank water from the stream, and came over to me every half hour or so to nuzzle me. He wasn't doing anything extraordinary, but every move he made was utterly elegant. That afternoon was almost perfect.

Unfortunately, in the back of my head I knew that when we got back to the barn Dr. Novegrad would be there with news. I'd been around horses long enough to be able to make an educated guess that the news wasn't going to be good.

Danny was waiting for me when we got back to Parkside. You know the beginning of a nightmare, the part before the monster is revealed or the weird stuff starts to happen, the part where your conscious mind is shouting *wake up!*— well, that's how it felt when I got to Mirage's stall. Actually, I had grown accustomed to feeling as though things could go terribly wrong at any moment. I was only just getting used to the fact that surprises weren't necessarily bad. After all, being with Danny had an element of the unknown to it, but I was learning to trust him and knew that everything was going to be okay. More than okay, even good.

Danny and Susan had cleaned up the stall, so Mirage had fresh hay, clean water, and a full bucket of carrots. They had even left his tack all neatly organized on the tack rack. It all looked much too neat.

"I can't believe you guys did all this," I said as I ran my hand over the gleaming bridle. They'd even polished his bit. "You shouldn't have."

If you want to know the truth, it kind of gave me the creeps. I kept thinking that if I could only wake up, then everything would be fine. Mirage would be healthy, the summer would just be beginning, and maybe my father would even still be there. The only part of that fantasy that I didn't like was that maybe Danny wouldn't be in that oh-so-perfect world. I knew that he was becoming very important to my happiness.

"No sweat. Anything for Mirage." Danny's false cheer was palpable.

"Yeah, we love Mirage, too, you know," Susan said. "Besides, once he gets back on his feet, it'll be nice to have everything like new. Right, Danny?"

For her sake, I tried to fake a smile. I thought I had done a pretty good job, but Danny obviously felt different.

"Does your stomach hurt?" he asked. "Your face looked funny all of a sudden. Like gas or something."

"I'm fine," I said, turning my back on him. Men!

We were all pacing around the stall when Dr. Novegrad came in. "Hello, folks," he greeted us quietly.

None of us said anything. We just looked at him.

"*Hmmm*. Looks as though I have four patients today." He tried to smile, hoping, I guess, that we would smile back. I wasn't the only one who was getting more and more frightened by the second.

Danny moved closer to me and put his arm around my shoulders as Dr. Novegrad cleared his throat. He wasn't smiling now.

"Okay," he said, "here's how it is, and I won't mince any words. It's serious. Mirage has osteogenic sarcoma."

I looked at Susan for help, but it was

clear she didn't have a clue as to what it meant either. I didn't really get scared until I looked at Danny. He was as white as a ghost and tears were forming in his eyes. Clearly, he understood what Dr. Novegrad was saying.

"Uh, what's that?" My voice came out in a whisper. I felt Danny's arm tighten around my shoulder.

Dr. Novegrad looked at Danny. Danny took a deep breath and turned me around so that he could look into my eyes. "Julia, it's cancer. Mirage has a malignant bone tumor."

I shook free of Danny's grasp and turned toward Dr. Novegrad. "No," I said to the doctor. What he was saying couldn't be true. I felt totally numb. "You can't know that. You didn't do enough tests," I argued. "You must be wrong."

Dr. Novegrad shook his head. "Julia, I'm sorry. I could run more tests, but the outcome won't be any different. Mirage has a malignant bone tumor. The operation, which probably wouldn't be successful, costs thousands of dollars," he said carefully. "My medical opinion is that it's too late to do anything to help him."

I could barely hear what he was saying, because the ringing in my ears was so loud.

"Julia." Dr. Novegrad sounded to me as if he were miles away. "Mirage is in a lot of discomfort, and as the pressure gets worse so will the pain. I recommend that you have him put down. It's the kindest thing you can do, under the circumstances."

I couldn't believe it. The only feeling I could compare it with was the way I had felt the morning my father left. That awful, scary, sinking feeling that things are about to spin out of control—the feeling that things will never, ever be the same again.

Actually, I think that those first moments in Mirage's stall were worse than the divorce. This time there was a terrible decision to be made, and the decision was mine.

When my dad left I had been relieved in some weird way. He and Mom had been screaming at each other for months, maybe years. Although I didn't know then what he'd done to make Mom so mad, at least I had someone, something, upon which to focus my anger. What Dr. Novegrad was saying didn't seem fair. It seemed so random, so out of left field. I just didn't know how to cope.

The blood rushed to my head. I couldn't hear anything or see anything that was happening around me. I was vaguely aware of Susan's hand on my arm, of the tightening of Danny's arm around my shoulders, and of Dr. Novegrad's concerned face, but it was as if it were all happening to someone else.

I knew that if I didn't get out of there and get away from everyone I would lose control. There would be time enough to deal with everyone later—and time enough to let them comfort me.

I remember shrugging off Danny's arm and smiling at Dr. Novegrad. Susan told me it was the scariest smile she'd ever seen outside of a horror movie. I also have a vague memory of thanking the doctor for his time and telling Danny I'd see him when he picked me up at seven that night. I don't remember anything else except standing on the pavement outside of Parkside, taking deep breaths in the hot August sunshine.

I started to run. I was running away from everything and everyone . . . away from Parkside, from Mirage, from Danny, from Susan, and most of all, from the truth and the awful decision that I had to make—a decision that only *I* could make.

Unfortunately, as the saying goes, "Wherever you go, there you are." In other words, no matter how hard I tried, I couldn't run away from myself.

CHAPTER

TEN

Mom was still at work when I got home. The little light on our answering machine looked as if it was having a seizure. I counted the flashes. There were seven messages. I didn't even bother to check to see who had called. It was funny. Although I didn't want to talk to anyone, the last thing I wanted was to be alone with my thoughts.

I went into the kitchen and opened the refrigerator door. I stood staring at the contents for a few minutes even though I wasn't the slightest bit hungry.

Something about the humming of our old Westinghouse was comforting. Weird, huh?

The ringing of the phone snapped me out of my trance and I screened the call on my answering machine. It was Danny calling to see if I was all right and to confirm our date.

I realized that I only had an hour to get ready. Suddenly our date became the most important, the only important, thing in my life. I know that sounds awful, what with the decision I had to make and all, but I guess I just wasn't ready to deal with what was happening to Mirage. Also, on some level, I knew that Mirage was already part of the past. Danny was part of my future, and therefore this date took on a new level of importance. It may not make sense, but that's how I felt.

I ran into my room and flipped on my stereo—loud. I mean extremely loud. The music drowned out any thoughts I had, and I let the ritual of getting ready for Danny take over.

I threw my boots in the corner and ripped off my britches and tank top.

Then I jumped into the hottest shower of my life. I didn't even feel it! I guess I wasn't feeling much of anything at that point. I took an extra long time shaving my legs and washing my hair.

How I looked became crucial to my survival. I wanted Danny to love me—to love me and never leave me. I guess I was focusing on the superficial element of what would make him do that. At least I felt I had some control over those elements.

Finally, I got out of the shower and, with my hair wrapped in a towel, began the torturous task of selecting my wardrobe for the evening. I still had no idea where Danny was taking me, but I knew how I wanted to look—hot. I didn't know what I would do if I lost him, so I was determined to do everything I could to make sure that didn't happen. I was scared about what that meant, but determined!

After trying on and discarding virtually everything in my closet and drawers, I ended up choosing a black miniskirt and a black silk tank top. I added a really cool black blazer with little cutouts on the sleeves that Laura had given me when her mother had taken her shopping for new clothes. Black pumps and some silver dangle earrings completed the outfit.

I'd never bothered much with makeup, but tonight I wanted to go wild. Luckily, my skin was temporarily zit free, so I put on blusher and mascara and went into Mom's bedroom to borrow some eye shadow. It took a couple of tries before I got it right, but by the time I added some Pink Passion lipstick and did some last-minute fussing with my hair, I was pleased with the result.

I was standing in front of the mirror and just staring at myself when Mom came in. It was unreal. The girl whose reflection I saw in the mirror was dressed to kill. She was all made up, and looked as if she didn't have a care in the world—except for the sad look in her eyes.

Mom, of course, saw right past the outfit and into the eyes.

"Oh, Julia. I'm so sorry."

"I don't want to talk about it, Mom."

"I think it's something you have to talk about. What did the doctor say?"

"He said . . ." I took a breath. "He

said Mirage should be put down," I continued. My throat felt so tight, I was surprised any words could squeeze out.

"Is there anything I can do?" she said, walking toward me.

I shook my head.

"Maybe—" she began.

"Look," I cut her off, "Danny will be here any minute. I need to be okay when he gets here. If I start to think about what the doctor said, I'll start crying. Please, Mom." I took her hand. "Just let it go for now. Okay?"

Before she could respond, I turned away. There would be time enough for all that later.

The doorbell rang. Talk about being saved by the bell. I made one final adjustment to my hair and opened the front door. I'll never forget the look on Danny's face.

"Oh, wow," he managed to say.

"What? I mean, hi." Not a great start.

"You look great. Are you okay?"

I looked at him until he realized how awful that sounded.

"I mean you always look great,"

Danny blurted out. "Tonight you look even better."

We were still standing in the open doorway. Danny smiled at me. "How about if we try this again—start all over. Hi, Julia, you look beautiful."

I smiled back at him. "Thanks."

"Listen, about earlier . . ."

"Not tonight. Okay?" I said quickly. "I don't want to think about Mirage, and I certainly don't want to talk about him. Please."

"Deal," Danny said, putting out his hand for me to shake. "Come on. Let's go."

Before we could escape, I heard my mother clearing her throat behind me. Time for introductions.

"Mom, Danny. Danny, my mom."

Danny stepped forward to shake my mother's hand. "It's a pleasure to meet you."

"Nice to meet you, too, Danny. I've heard so much about you."

The predictability of this conversation was enough to make me gag. I wasn't up for the traditional formalities, so I grabbed Danny's hand, and said, "We gotta go, Mom. I'll see you, uh, later."

Normally, Mom would have stopped me to ask where I was going and exactly when I'd be home, but that night I guess she figured it would be a good idea to cut me some slack.

I practically pulled Danny out of the apartment and closed the door behind me. When we were alone on the landing, I turned to him and smiled. "Where are we going?" Suddenly, I noticed the picnic basket at his feet.

He grinned. "Your rooftop!" He held out his arm for me to take. "Your ladyship."

I curtsied and slipped my arm through his, and we climbed the stairs to the roof.

Danny had brought blankets for us to sit on and as I gazed out over Central Park, he laid out an unbelievable feast. He unpacked fresh roast beef, smoked turkey, four different cheeses, fruit, and freshly baked French bread. It was awesome.

We dug in and, for a while, the process of gorging ourselves took the place of conversation. After we'd completely stuffed ourselves, we leaned back against the chimney, sipping glasses of sparkling apple cider. Danny kept trying to make conversation, but I just wasn't responding. I mean I answered him, but "yes," "no," and "I don't know" hardly count as a real dialogue.

I guess I was so wrapped up in myself that I didn't realize that I was being rude. Actually, I was also getting nervous. There I was, with a guy I liked a lot, all alone on the roof. On the one hand, I wanted something to happen. On the other hand, I really wasn't feeling up to it. As much as I had tried to keep Mirage out of my mind, he was still lingering there in the back of it, making me sad.

After a few minutes of silence Danny jumped to his feet. "This was a bad idea," he said.

I looked up, shocked. "What?"

"I can tell you want to be alone." He didn't sound mad, just hurt. I knew he wanted me to open up to him.

He started to throw what was left of the food back into the basket, and I started to cry. The tears seemed to come from nowhere.

"Oh, Julia. Don't."

Danny wrapped his arms around me, and I sobbed and sobbed into his chest. I didn't know if I was going to be able to stop—ever—and I didn't care. Danny held me, rocked me, and stroked my hair until my tears were spent.

"I'm sorry," I managed to say through the tears. "Really, this has been the best celebration I've ever been to. I'm so-o-o glad you're here," I sobbed. I'm having a great time."

"Yeah, I can tell," he said with a smile as he tilted my face toward his.

I managed a weak smile in response. "It's just that I'm so scared."

"It's okay. You can talk to me, Julia."

I rearranged myself more comfortably in his arms. "It's just that everything in my life keeps changing," I began. "First my dad left, and I had to get used to that. I realized how poor we really were, at least compared with before, and I had to adjust. Then, just when I was getting used to having Mirage and Susan as my only friends, you came along." I smiled at him. "I guess I'm still getting used to that part. And now," I paused, "Mirage is

197

sick, and I don't want to get used to that. I just can't find anything to be happy about right now."

Danny's arms held me tighter.

"Anything but you, that is." What I didn't say was that along with the happiness he brought came some fear.

"I don't mind Penny and the rest not really being my friends," I said, "but you're going back to school next week and everything is awful." I had to stop talking, the sobs were coming so hard and fast.

Danny held me for a minute longer and then pulled me away from his chest. He cupped my chin in his hand. "Look, Penny, Laura, and Denise are not worth crying about. Mirage is."

I started to hiccough and I could feel the tears running down my cheeks. Danny reached out and wiped them away. "But," he said, "why are you crying about me? You'll be coming up for orientation a couple of days after I get up to Delany. I told you, you'll only be about ten minutes away from me. We'll be able to see each other all the time. If you want to, that is."

I smiled at Danny through my tears. "I do."

Danny leaned forward and kissed me on the lips. He started to pull away, but I leaned into the kiss and felt his tongue gently run over my lips. Suddenly, our embrace grew stronger and we kissed in a way I had never kissed before. All these feelings welled up inside of me.

At that moment, there was nothing I didn't want to do. All I could think of was getting closer to Danny than I'd ever been to another human being. I didn't want to lose him, and even though he had never pressured me to go all the way, I wanted to.

His hands on my back felt wonderful. I shrugged out of my blazer, and our kisses grew deeper. He cradled my head in his strong hands, and I began to pull my tank top out of the waistband of my skirt.

I felt his hand reach down and grab my wrist.

"Don't," he insisted. His voice was hoarse.

I pulled back. "Why?" I could feel my lips tingling. "Don't you want to?"

Abruptly, Danny stood up. He shoved

his hands into the pockets of his jeans and walked to the edge of the roof and then back to where I was sitting. "Of course I want to. You're beautiful, absolutely beautiful, and I care about you so much. But"—he paused for a second—". . . uh, you've never made love before, have you?"

I shook my head. For some stupid reason I was embarrassed.

Danny knelt down beside me. "Look, this isn't what you need right now. You don't really want to do this." I began to protest that I did, that I was ready, but he silenced me with a gentle kiss and sat down. He pulled me to him so that my head was on his strong chest.

"Julia, don't think this is something I don't want to do. I just want it to be perfect, to be right for both of us. What you need right now is to be held, not, well, you know. I'm not going anywhere."

I started to cry again, only this time it was out of total embarrassment. I felt as if I had made a complete fool out of myself.

Danny held me for a minute and then continued. "We'll have plenty of time to let things take their natural course up at school." I looked up into his eyes. "We can afford to wait," he said. "It's going to be wonderful."

We stayed on the roof for a while longer. We talked about what it was going to be like when we got up to school. We talked about studying together, meeting his friends, going to poetry readings, all the normal, everyday things that two college kids in love talk about. And, for those few precious moments on the roof, that's all I allowed myself to feel like: a normal college kid in love.

Mom was asleep when I got back to the apartment, so I quietly got ready for bed. As I lay there, trying to doze off, I thought about Mirage. But my final thought, the one that sent me into my dreams with a big smile, was how lucky I was to have found Danny, and how much we had to look forward to together.

CHAPTER

ELEVEN

Although I went to sleep thinking about Danny, I was awakened by the reality of what was going to happen to Mirage. I knew that I had to have him put to sleep. The longer I waited, the harder the decision was going to be.

I lay in bed, hoping that if I didn't get up, maybe nothing would change. I heard the phone ringing, and my mom answering it. A moment later there was a knock at my door.

"Julia," Mom said, poking her head in. "Sweetheart, phone's for you."

I wasn't exactly in the mood to talk to anyone. "Mom, tell them that . . ."

"Julia!" Her voice was harsh. "Take the phone."

Mothers can be strange sometimes, so I just got up and took it.

"Hello," I said.

There was a moment's silence on the other end.

"Hello!"

"Hi, Jules." It was a man's voice; it was my dad.

Now I was the one who was silent.

"Julia? Are you there?"

I had this awful feeling in my stomach. Anger, excitement, fear—you name it, I felt it. "Who is this?" I demanded. Of course, I already knew who it was.

"It's your father, Julia."

"Oh." I didn't know what else to say.

"How are you?" He didn't sound as if he knew what to say, either.

"Why are you calling?" The excitement part was dimming. The anger part was taking the lead.

"Julia, honey, I know it's been a while . . ."

"Like two years."

"Uh, yes." He paused. "Your mother called me last night and told me about Mirage. I'm so sorry."

"She had no right to call you," I yelled into the receiver.

"She had every right!" Now he started to sound angry. "I'm your father. I care about you, you know."

I laughed into the phone. "I could tell from all the calls and visits you've made."

"I just want to help—"

"No, thanks," I interrupted. "It's too late for that. You could have been helping all along. I don't need you now!"

I slammed down the phone and ran into Mom's room. She was sitting on the bed with her head in her hands. She looked up as I came in.

"How could you!" I shouted.

"Julia . . ."

"We're fine without him! He has nothing to do with my life. How could you have called him?"

"Stop it!" she ordered. "I thought you might need to talk to him. About Mirage. I thought you might want to." Then she started to cry.

"Oh, Mom," I said, sitting down next to her on the bed.

"I thought you might need some comfort," she confessed. "I thought—"

"It's okay, Mom," I interrupted. "I do need comfort. But not from him." It was kind of a turning point for me. I had thought, in some small part of my brain, that if only my dad were around, things would be different. I knew then, however, that what I really needed, he didn't have to give.

"Do you want me to come with you to the stable?" Mom offered.

"No, thanks," I said. "I gotta get going."

I went back to my room, dressed, and purposefully left the house. I was in the street in front of Parkside by 8:30 A.M. The stable doesn't really open for business until 9:00 A.M. on weekends, but the night watchman was still on duty and he let me in.

When I got to the top of the ramp I whistled for Mirage, who whinnied back at me. As I walked to his stall, I didn't let myself think about the fact that this was going to be the last time he ever did that

—or that I would never sit astride him again.

Bending under the chain, I started to talk to Mirage in low, soothing tones. "You know you're my best friend, don't you?" He nuzzled me as if he understood my words. "And I'm only doing this for your own good. You don't want to be in pain, do you?" Mirage pawed the ground. He was tired of small talk; he wanted his breakfast.

I went down to the end of the aisle and got a huge bucket of chopped-up apples and carrots. When I got back to the stall, I found Susan handing Mirage sugar lumps.

"Hi," I said.

"You're going to do it, aren't you?" she asked. I put my arms around her and we hugged for a few minutes. I held on to her tightly. Somehow, comforting her made me feel a little better.

"Yep," I answered. "When Dr. Novegrad gets here, I'm going to have Mirage put to sleep." It was the first time I had said it out loud. Before I could cry I said, "Come on, let's groom him."

I don't know why, but for some reason

it soothed me to stand in the stall with Susan, saying nothing. We ran our brushes over and over his coat. Then we cleaned his hooves and braided his mane.

Susan decided to give me some time alone with Mirage, so she went down to the mounting block.

"I love you," I said as I rubbed Mirage's scratch spot. He stuck out his neck and wiggled his lips at me. I had to laugh.

Penny and Denise came by a little while later. Susan must have told them what was going on. Even though I was still mad at them about the party, I knew that they really cared about Mirage, too. When Laura arrived, she ran over to her tack box and pulled out some red ribbon and started braiding Mirage's tail.

Finally, Danny came upstairs with Susan. He gave me a kiss and put his arms around me. "You're doing the right thing, you know," he assured me.

I couldn't believe I hadn't broken down yet, but the feel of Danny's arms around me almost pushed me over the edge. I carefully disengaged from his embrace.

"I'm here if you need me," he said. "Now or later."

I managed a weak smile, but it didn't last long. I could hear Dr. Novegrad coming up the ramp to the stalls.

Everyone turned to look at me as Dr. Novegrad came around the corner. He stopped in his tracks when he saw the crowd gathered around Mirage's stall. "Julia . . ." He nodded at everyone and then he asked, "Have you made a decision?"

"Yes." I took a deep breath. "I think we should put Mirage to sleep. Today. Now." I was really surprised at how steady my voice was. I knew that I never would have been able to make that decision three months earlier.

Dr. Novegrad set his bag on a bale of hay and took off his jacket. I looked at my friends, who by now were huddled together crying and sobbing.

"Uh, you guys . . ." I said. "Listen, I really want to be alone when this happens."

"Come on, everyone. Let's go," Danny said. He led the group away.

I went over to Mirage and rested my

cheek against his neck. His coat felt soft and comforting against my skin.

Dr. Novegrad came over and put his hands on my shoulders. "Are you sure you want to be here for this?" he asked.

"He's my horse," I said. "It's my decision to put him down, and I'll stay with him till it's over." I took a deep, ragged breath.

"Good for you. He'll feel no pain, you know."

Dr. Novegrad went over to his bag and took out a small glass vial and a syringe. He inserted the needle into the vial and drew off the necessary medication before putting the vial back in his bag. I felt that I needed to watch everything he was doing, sort of like when you pass a really bad traffic accident. You know you should look away, but some weird force draws your eyes to the mangled cars.

Then, grabbing some alcohol and cotton, he walked over to where I was cradling Mirage's head. He knelt down and began talking very soothingly as he stroked Mirage's neck.

"All right, boy, this isn't going to hurt," Dr. Novegrad said, finding a vein for the injection. "Now, just relax, Mirage."

Mirage received the injection that would put him to sleep forever in a vein just below his neck. "It won't be long now," the doctor said, as he stood up. "I'm going to let you two be alone now."

My eyes were too filled with tears to be able to see him leave.

I stood stroking Mirage's neck and head as he began to tremble. He whinnied a couple of times, knelt down, and rolled onto his side. I was sobbing so hard I couldn't breathe, but I sat in the hay and lifted his head onto my lap.

I don't know how long we were like that. Finally Mirage opened his eyes, looked at me, and shuddered one last time. Then he was gone.

The next thing I remember was Danny beside me stroking my hair and cradling me in his arms. We sat there a while longer before Danny helped me stand up.

"Your mom is waiting downstairs," he said.

"Not yet." I sobbed into his shoulder. "I'm not ready yet."

He held me in Mirage's stall until I had

cried myself out. When I looked up into his face, he had tears streaming down his cheeks. I knew how much he really cared. Even though I'd lost Mirage, I'd found something else that could be as wonderful.

CHAPTER

TWELVE

"Ithaca!" The conductor's voice boomed over the loudspeaker. "Everyone out who's getting out!" I frantically started to pack up my knapsack and gather my stuff, as I looked out the window and saw the station come into view.

Already? I thought. *I can't believe I'm here.* The train ride to college had turned out just like the summer . . . over before I realized what was happening.

The train had come to a halt by the time I rose from my seat. I reached up and grabbed the bags from the overhead rack as the porter came into the car and walked down the aisle toward me.

"Give you a hand with your bags, miss?" he asked. He smiled, seeing me struggle with all my luggage.

"Thanks, I'd appreciate it."

The porter grabbed hold of the two large bags and lifted them as though he were carrying two pillows. I followed him down the aisle to the doorway of the car.

"Watch your step, now," he warned.

I carefully walked down the stairs and onto the platform. Then I reached into my pocket and pulled out a couple dollar bills.

"Here you are," I said to the porter. "Thanks."

The porter took the money and tipped his cap. "Thank you, ma'am. Is someone meeting you here?"

"I don't know," I said, looking around the platform quickly. "It doesn't look like it."

He saw the hurt in my eyes. "Well, have a good stay, miss."

The porter turned on his heel and climbed back into the train. I stood there squinting into the late-afternoon sun and watched as the train began moving slowly out of the station. Within a few moments all I could see were the lights on the last car fading in the distance.

I took a deep breath and sighed. My eyes began to fill with tears as I realized, quite suddenly, how very much alone I felt for the first time since Mirage's death. Although Danny had left for school the following day, Mom and Susan had made sure, in spite of my protestations, that I was not left alone except when I was sleeping. Actually, Susan slept over at my apartment every night.

I wished Danny had been able to be here with me now. Let's face it, I wished *anyone* were here to meet me.

"Come on," I said to myself. "Haven't you learned anything this summer?"

I adjusted my backpack and reached down to pick up the other bags that the porter had deposited. As I was bending down, I stopped suddenly as something caught my eye. A tall man was coming out of a door at the far end of the platform.

I squinted as I tried to make him out.

As he got closer, I recognized the familiar-looking figure and walk. "You made it!" I shouted. Chalk up another point for obviousness!

I stood frozen as the man stopped, looked in my direction, and then began running faster and faster toward me. I immediately dropped my bags and began running toward him as fast as I could.

"Julia!" Danny cried as he reached me and took me in his strong arms. "I can't believe how much I missed you."

Tears of joy streamed down my face. "I haven't been able to think of anyone or anything else but you since I left the city," I told him.

"I'm so glad you're finally here," Danny said, kissing me.

It was like a scene out of a movie. I was so happy, and I felt so safe in his arms. I never wanted him to let go of me.

"Come on," Danny said as he bent to pick up my two bags. "I have my roommate's car outside. We'll drop your stuff off at the dorm and go grab a bite to eat. Then we'll get you settled in." I held on to his arm as we walked through the station and out the doorway toward the parking lot.

Danny led the way to the car. He put the bags in the trunk before unlocking the door and holding it open for me. I got in and Danny went around to the driver's side, unlocked his door, and got into the car.

As he put the key in the ignition, I put my hand on his. He turned toward me, and we looked deeply into each other's eyes.

"Thank you for making these last few weeks so bearable," I said. "I don't think I could have survived without you there by my side."

Uncontrollably, the tears began streaming down my cheeks.

Danny reached into his pocket for his handkerchief. He held it out as he grinned at me. "Dry up, kiddo. There's no need for tears up here."

I took the handkerchief and looked up into Danny's blue eyes.

"You're right," I agreed. "But if we're going to be up here together for the next few years, you're gonna have to feed me . . . and I mean soon. I'm starving!"

Danny sat up straight and gave a mock salute. "Yes, ma'am!"

"Ya know, I think I'm in the mood for a burger. How about you?"

"Your wish is my command," he said, starting the car.

As we pulled out of the parking lot Danny put his arm around my shoulder and we headed toward a burger, fries, and whatever else the future held in store for us.

CHOOSE ME

MARILYN KAYE

"I like Hope," Maria said. "She seems fun."

It was the next morning, and the two girls were at Nicole's kitchen table, working on a sociology project. "It's strange, though," Maria continued. "No one seems to know anything about her. You know Elaine Travers? She hangs out with Hope, and she told me Hope never talks about her old school or her old friends. There's something mysterious about her. What do you think?"

Nicole looked up. "Huh?"

"You haven't heard a word I've said," Maria said accusingly.

"Sorry," Nicole replied. "I guess my mind is somewhere else."

Maria immediately became sympathetic. "You're thinking about Martin again, aren't you?"

Nicole got up and began pacing around the kitchen. "I don't know what to do, Maria. He's acting weirder and weirder."

"Do you think there's a problem at home?" Maria wondered. "A fight with his parents, maybe?"

"No, he'd tell me about that. We always talk about family stuff. I know it has something to do with homecoming—that he wants to protect me from being hurt. But the more I think about it, it doesn't make sense. He knows I'm not that wimpy."

Thinking about it was giving Nicole a headache. She needed a distraction.

"Hey, I haven't shown you my dress!"

Maria's eyes lit up. "You got a dress for homecoming already?"

"Yeah. Stay here, and I'll go put it on." She ran up to her room, and took the pink creation out of her closet. She undressed and slipped it on. For a second she debated putting on make-up too, so Maria could get the full effect, but she didn't want to take too long. She *did* rummage through her closet for a pair of high-heeled pumps, though.

Wobbling a bit on the shoes she hadn't worn in ages, she started out. But she stopped when she noticed a gaudy cardboard crown hanging on her bedpost, a souvenir from last year's Halloween party. She snatched it up and stuck it on her head.

She felt every inch a queen as she sauntered into the kitchen. And Maria's reaction was perfect. She gasped, then she screeched. "It's absolutely gorgeous! Nick, you look like you've just been crowned Miss America!"

Nicole struck a pose and spoke in a high, squeaky voice: "My greatest ambition in life is to use my title to bring peace to all nations." Her speech was interrupted by the sound of the doorbell. "That's probably Mom, forgetting her keys again."

But it wasn't. "Martin! Come on in." Nicole was surprised to see him. It wasn't like him to come over without calling first.

Martin was staring at her, and she remembered what she was wearing. She giggled. "It's my dress for homecoming. I was showing it off to Maria." His reaction wasn't anything like Maria's.

"You don't like it," she said flatly.

He shrugged. "Isn't it a little too . . . revealing?"

Nicole was beginning to lose her patience. "Martin, would you *please* let me know what's bothering you? These moods you're having are driving me straight up the wall! We have to *talk*."

At that moment, Maria walked in, catching Nicole's words. She tiptoed back into the kitchen and then returned, carrying her books. "Hi, Martin. Nicole, I've got to go. I'll call you later."

Alone with Martin, Nicole steeled herself. She had no idea what was coming, but from his miserable expression, she knew it was going to be major. "Do you want to sit down?"

He shook his head. "I'm sorry about what I said about your dress. It's . . . well, you look spectacular." But he said it with so much sadness, Nicole couldn't even say thank you. She just waited.

"I know I've been acting like a real

jerk," he said. "And I'm sorry about that too."

"I'm not angry about that," Nicole replied. "I'm worried. Martin, what's going on?"

"It's this homecoming thing. Nicole, it's going to change everything. I feel like I'm going to lose you."

Nicole gaped. "What are you talking about? Why would you lose me?"

"You saw what went on last night at Pizza Palace. You're going to have every guy in the senior class coming on to you. Especially if you win."

"That's crazy!" Nicole burst out. "I'm not interested in any other guy. What's made you feel so insecure all of a sudden?"

"I'm not insecure," Martin said. "I'm just being realistic." He paused. "Nicole, you're the only girl I've ever cared about. Two years ago, when I first asked you out, I was amazed when you said yes. I've never stopped being amazed that I'm lucky enough to have you as a girlfriend. Okay, maybe I *am* insecure."

"You're being silly," Nicole said. "This isn't like you!"

"*I'm* being silly? You're the one who's taking all this nonsense seriously. And that's not like *you*."

Nicole's head was spinning. "Martin, I'm the same person I've always been. You're the one who's making the big deal about it. To me, it's just, I don't know, *fun*. That's all."

"Then if you don't think it's a big deal . . ."

"What?"

"Drop out."

Nicole was dumbfounded. "What?"

"Withdraw your name. Don't be a candidate."

"Why—why should I do that?"

"Because I don't like it!" Martin's face was becoming red. "I don't like all these guys flirting with you. You say you love me. If you really love me, you'll forget about being homecoming queen."

Nicole stared at him in disbelief. "I don't know what to say."

His eyes were pleading. "We have a relationship. I thought you cared—"

"Of course I care!" Nicole interrupted. "But you're making an issue out of something that has nothing to do with our relationship. You talk about *me* changing. *You're* the one who's changing."

"Nicole, do you remember that racist demonstration in San Francisco last year? And I wanted to march in the counterdemonstration? You didn't want me to do it because it was going to be dangerous. So I didn't."

"Martin, that's an entirely different situation."

His frustration was clearly evident. "Look, all I know is this. I don't want you to be homecoming queen. Just . . . think about it, okay? That's all I'm asking. Think about it."

There was an enormous lump in Nicole's throat. But somehow she managed to whisper, "I'll think about it."

He nodded. "I'll see you tomorrow."

As soon as he left, Nicole sank into a chair. She couldn't remember ever feeling so confused. This demand of his wasn't rational. It wasn't logical. Think about it, he said. What was there to think about? She could think for weeks, and it still wouldn't make any sense.

Finally, aware that she was probably wrinkling her dress, she rose heavily and started up the stairs. In her room she began unzipping the dress. Her eyes drifted down to a framed photograph on her dresser. There she was with Martin at a cookout last summer. She remembered the day so clearly. They'd wandered away from the party and sat by themselves as the sun went down, talking about their hopes, their dreams. Oh, she loved him, and she didn't want to lose him. If homecoming really bothered him so much . . .

Then she caught a glimpse of herself in the mirror. She still had that silly crown on her head. The sight of it brought back her private fantasies, the giddy pleasure she'd been feeling since her nomination.

She jerked her head up. What right did he have to ask this of her? Why should she give in to his ridiculous insecurity? What about *her* hopes, *her* dreams?

She finished unzipping the dress. Then, very carefully, she put it on the padded hanger and placed it in the front of her closet. She *would* be wearing it again.

* * *

She arrived at school early on Monday, and stationed herself by Martin's locker. She knew he had a meeting that morning, and he always stopped at his locker first.

She felt surprisingly calm. In the back of her mind, there was the faint hope that he had already realized how silly he was being. If not—well, maybe she could still convince him.

He was coming down the hall. She smiled at him, putting all the warmth and affection she felt into her smile. He smiled back, but his smile was wary.

"Hi," she said.

He echoed, "Hi."

There was a pause. Then she said, "Well?"

And he replied, "It's your move."

Her heart sank. So he hadn't changed his mind. And with a dull realization, she knew she wouldn't be able to change it for him. She fixed her eyes on his collar, afraid that if she watched his face, she'd lose her nerve. "I've thought about what you said, and I think . . . I think you have to have faith in me. I love you, and nothing's going to change that." She took a deep breath. "I'm not dropping out, Martin."

She forced herself to look directly at him. There was enormous sadness in his eyes, but he spoke stiffly. "Maybe it's for the best. We've been going out for a long time, and we should start seeing other people."

Desperately holding back her tears, Nicole whispered, "If that's what you want."

"It seems to be what *you* want," Martin murmured. He turned and started away.

"Martin?"

He turned back. The hall was filling with students, so she hurried forward to join him. "You said you'd escort me at homecoming, remember? I'm holding you to that."

He nodded slightly. And then he disappeared into the crowd.

"Nicole?"

Her vision was blurry, and she could barely make out Kristie's face. "Yes?"

"Could we get together and talk about the Thanksgiving food drive?"

"I can't now. I have to be somewhere. Later, okay?"

Hurrying around the corner, she went into the school newspaper office.

The other candidates, Courtney, Hope, and Melissa, were already there. "Hope I'm not late," Nicole said.

"You're right on time," a girl holding a camera told her. "Why don't you stand over here, by Hope." She stepped back and examined the group. "No, you and you change places." She tried several different poses. "Sorry about this, but I want to get one really good shot for the newspaper. Yes, I think this is nice."

She stepped back and began focusing her camera. "Okay, everyone. Smile!"

Nicole did as she was told. But it wasn't easy.

Dear Readers,

When I was eighteen years old I was lucky enough to go to college right in the heart of New York City. During my freshman year I started horseback riding at the Claremont Stables and, by the end of my junior year, I was one of the teachers!

I always envied the teenage girls who had grown up in New York and who kept horses of their own at the stable. It seemed to me the best of both worlds: city life and country fun.

Things are not, however, always as they seem. What looks like the perfect life from the outside can be really tough sometimes for the person living it. Julia finds that out—that sometimes you can't have everything you want, and that part of growing up is taking responsibility and making decisions . . . even really tough ones.

Still, as Julia discovers, although making hard decisions is part of being an adult, there is a lot of fun that goes along with it as well.

I really hope you enjoy Julia's story.
Best wishes and happy trails,

Mallory Stevens

📖 HarperPaperbacks *By Mail*

Read all of the
Changes ROMANCES

Discover yourself in the dramatic stories of the Changes heroines as they face the same hopes and fears as you.

MAIL TO: Harper Collins Publishers
P.O.Box 588, Dunmore, PA 18512-0588
TELEPHONE: 1-800-331-3716
(Visa and Mastercard holders!)
YES, please send me the following titles:

Changes Romances
- ❏ #1 My Phantom Love (0-06-106770-9) $3.50
- ❏ #2 Looking Out for Lacey (0-06-106772-5) $3.50
- ❏ #3 The Unbelievable Truth (0-06-106774-1) $3.50
- ❏ #4 Runaway (0-06-106782-2) $3.50
- ❏ #5 Cinderella Summer (0-06-106776-8)............$3.50

Mollie Fox Mysteries
- ❏ #1 First to Die (0-06-106100-X) $3.50
- ❏ #2 Double Dose (0-06-106101-8).....................$3.50

The Vampire Diaries
- ❏ Vol. I The Awakening (0-06-106097-6)............$3.99
- ❏ Vol. II The Struggle (0-06-106098-4)...............$3.99
- ❏ Vol. III The Fury (0-06-106099-2)...................$3.99
- ❏ Vol. IV Dark Reunion (0-06-106775-X) $3.99

Freshman Dorm
- ❏ #1 Freshman Dorm (0-06-106000-3)................$3.50
- ❏ #15 Freshman Heartbreak (0-06-106140-9)......$3.50
- ❏ #16 Freshman Feud (0-06-106141-7) $3.50
- ❏ #17 Freshman Follies (0-06-106142-5) $3.50

SUBTOTAL ....$_____
POSTAGE AND HANDLING* ....$ 2.00
SALES TAX (Add applicable state sales tax) ....$_____

TOTAL: $_____
(Remit in U.S. funds. Do not send cash.)

NAME_____
ADDRESS_____
CITY _____
STATE_____ ZIP _____

Allow up to six weeks for delivery. Prices subject to change.
Valid only in U.S. and Canada.

*Free postage/handling if you buy four or more!

H0341